A KINGDOM
FAR AND CLEAR

A KINGDOM FAR AND CLEAR

THE COMPLETE SWAN LAKE TRILOGY

MARK HELPRIN

ILLUSTRATED BY
CHRIS VAN ALLSBURG

CALLA EDITIONS
ARIEL BOOKS

Swan Lake:
Text copyright © 1989 by Mark Helprin
Illustrations copyright © 1989 by Chris Van Allsburg

A City in Winter:
Text copyright © 1996 by Mark Helprin
Illustrations copyright © 1996 by Chris Van Allsburg

The Veil of Snows:
Text copyright © 1997 by Mark Helprin
Illustrations copyright © 1997 by Chris Van Allsburg

Second Calla Edition

A Kingdom Far and Clear: The Complete Swan Lake Trilogy, first published by Calla Editions in 2010, is an unabridged republication in one volume of *Swan Lake*, originally published in 1989 by Ariel Books, Houghton Mifflin Company, Boston; *A City in Winter*, originally published in 1996 by Viking, New York; and *The Veil of Snows*, originally published in 1997 by Viking, New York. The text has been completely reset and redesigned for this edition, and the artist has provided one additional black and white illustration (page 199).

International Standard Book Number
ISBN-13: 978-1-60660-012-2
ISBN-10: 1-60660-012-5

Manufactured in the United States by Courier Corporation
CALLA EDITIONS
An imprint of Dover Publications, Inc.
60012501
www.callaeditions.com

For Alexandra and Olivia
M .H.

The Contents

Swan Lake   1

A City in Winter   85

The Veil of Snows   199

THE PLATES

SWAN LAKE

"The forest was in its own way inviolable — a domain of hearth
   smoke in unwavering columns against a flawless blue sky."   3

"He was moved and proud to see her sitting in a corner of the porch,
   recovering from the heat, with streaks of salt on her sunburned face."   9

"They brought me to a white-bearded bald old fellow who was
   lying on a worn Turkoman carpet in front of a half-dead fire."   17

"They, the Damavand, are wedded to their horses and appear to
   grow out of their saddles."   23

"As the lead bowman flung open his shutters, the others
   followed suit."   29

"When he was older, I set up a camp in the forest, where we went
   in the greatest secrecy for military training."   39

"There were indoor hunting preserves."   43

"Each pig had a groom and two handlers, and lived in a big
   bedroom with *trompe l'oeil* depictions of an oak forest."   45

"Thousands of cloud-white swans were rising on a column
   of blue air."   51

"The swans were dancing in a ring."   53

"She was dressed in black, as if to say, 'Judge me by myself alone.'"   63

"He jumped to his feet, bow in hand, and stepped forward."   71

"They fell as if they knew how to take to the air."   79

"They filled the sky—two swans, wings extended, riding on the
   air and powering themselves ahead."   83

XI

A City in Winter

"I lived in the mountains, I knew war."   87

"I hungered for the sight of a great thing."   95

"A single couple might be seen, skating together through the
    shadows."   101

"By the light of a myrrh fire they gave me soup and bread."   107

"He wore a mask that made him look like death itself."   117

"I spun gently on the rope and passed window after window."   127

"Please forgive one who is lower than the slave of a slave."   135

"The fires of a hundred thousand ovens were twinkling in the
    distance."   141

"Laden with peonies, I walked slowly toward my station."   153

"I can see the clock tower at this very moment."   163

"I was in a vast room at the base of thirty stories of gleaming
    machinery."   167

"Astrahn and Notorincus were led to a tiny filth-encrusted hole
   in a back wall."   179

"They said that as he fell he flew."   191

"And the millions in the square fell silent."   197

THE VEIL OF SNOWS

"In my room, on a shelf, is a blue bottle."   201

"I was so afraid that my heels shook as if in an earthquake."   209

"Notorincus saw that I glanced repeatedly at the cooks."   213

"She held her baby up in the air, moving him to and fro until he
    smiled with the game."   221

"The Tookisheims were absolutely tickled to be in the presence
    of the queen, and they gushed, burped, bloated, and moaned."   229

"I went to the parapet and looked over the dizzying sides of
    moonlit stone."   235

"Immediately before me was a child in homespun cotton
    encrusted with ice."   239

"She held herself stock still for a moment that proved to be the
    last instant of the old era."   247

"On the rooftops we built a garden so vast you could not see the
    end of it in any direction."   255

"And, with their machines, what did they throw? … Dead
    animals infected with plague."   261

"Her soldiers would be incalculably vigilant and hard-fighting
    if they knew she was among them, with neither plate nor mail."   273

"And then I saw a huge sword rise in the air behind her."   289

"I walked slowly and confidently, trying to stay the horse from
    movement by imagining how I would seize the bridle."   293

"And then I saw them, father and son, riding together."   299

BOOK ONE
SWAN LAKE

nce, the mountains held within their silvered walls a forest so high and so gracefully forgotten that it rode above the troubles of the world as easily as the blinding white clouds that sometimes catch on jagged peaks and musically unfurl. Cold lakes scattered in the greenery ran so deep that soundings were of no avail, and the meadows along the tree line, suspended in the light, were as smooth and green as slabs of jade.

Here birds sought refuge from hunters on the plain, and found higher realms in tranquillity and perfection. And though empires and kingdoms below might nervously claim it, the forest was in its own way inviolable — a domain of hearth smoke in unwavering columns against a flawless blue sky, of mountains clad in wind-buffed ice, of the thinnest air, of rivers running white and bursting with oxygen.

Perhaps you have felt the presence of such places when, in a darkened concert hall, the music makes the moon rise, perfectly fresh and bright, as if the roof has opened up above you, or when the trees shudder in a sudden wind and the sun unexpectedly lights the undersides of their rustling leaves. They do exist, although they are so hard to find that it is tempting to believe they are illusions. But all places cannot be exactly the same. Some are slightly better than others; some are much better; some are vastly better. Were the world uniform, you would not be able to distinguish a pin from a needle. But you can, of course. And what about a pin and a hippopotamus? And that is just the beginning. As for those who would deny the existence of forests hidden in a crown of mountains, of sheltered places, of charged land-scapes that can put together broken hearts, or at least keep them from shattering into pieces, ask them about hippopotamuses and pins.

The forest was a place of exile for an old man and a little girl. She believed that her mother and father were still on the plain below, caught up in struggles she could hardly imagine. Though she did not remember them, she loved them, and had just reached an age when she wanted, most of all, to join them. Because the old man under-stood that she knew little but her childhood, he thought to tell her something of the world that she was determined to see.

This was long ago, and in many ways the time was so different that you would hardly know it, except in your heart — for your heart is quick and right to tell you that all things that matter are more or less the same as they have been and will be, and that however young you are, however happy you may be, somehow you know them, some-how you know sadness; somehow, you have been there.

The old man often told the little girl stories as she lay in her bed in a tiny room lined with fragrant cedar. Stories had been something to dream upon. But this one was for the full light, and he wanted to tell it, and did, on a late summer afternoon when the roses were hot and completely unbound, and the hay stood in dry blond-ing sheaves.

They had been working since dawn. They were exhausted. Never had she questioned the hard labor, winter or summer, and she had always risen and retired with the sun. But he had known girls, with eyes just as blue, and flaxen hair, who hadn't ever worked a minute and hadn't ever thought they would. Because of this, he was apologetic when she labored beside him, which made her think only that he was kind. She realized, after all, that the milk she drank and the cheese she ate came from their cows, and that the cows ate the hay that she cut and carried. Thus the work appeared to her to be justified not only by custom but by economics.

Still, he was moved and proud to see her sitting in a corner of the porch, recovering from the heat, with streaks of salt on her sun-burned face. Although she had been through storms, blizzards, and dark days, and although she knew loneliness, cold, and hunger, she had never encountered deception, malice, or greed, and was sure that if she did she could easily defeat them. Her confidence showed in her pure and open expression.

"Do you still think about descending to the plain to look for your mother and father?" he asked, because, especially now, he did not want her to leave.

"Yes," she answered.

"All right," he said. "Next year, at the beginning of summer, I'll send you down with Anna."

"Who will help with the harvest?" she asked.

"I can do it myself. Anna will take you. Besides, by harvest time you might even be back."

"Why don't *you* take me? Why do I have to go with Anna? I don't want to go with her. Her eyes refuse to look at anything but the end of her broom."

"Don't say that about Anna. It's not kind. Anyway, I can't go down there."

"Why not?"

"I don't want to."

"Don't want to, or can't?"

"Both. As you get older," he said, "they tend to merge. You tire of some things, and most of all of repeating them — either in action or in thought. I would grow impossibly tired of reliving my life there. Here, I don't have to replot all my battles."

"But you did great things," she insisted. "You knew the emperor. Anna told me you did."

"Anna should never have spoken about that."

"Isn't it true?"

"Yes, I knew the emperor. But he is the emperor no longer, and though the people surrounding him thought they shared in his glory, they woke up to find that they had been eating ashes. My life was a failure, until I came here and unsaddled myself of ambition."

"How old were you then?"

"Almost sixty."

She looked at him blankly, unable to imagine the passing of sixty years.

"Perhaps you should know a little of what occurred in my life before you were born," he said, "now that you want to go down there, where things are so different."

As he began to speak she folded her knees up against her chest and rested her chin on them in perfect comfort, with the flexibility of those under ten. The crickets were singing in the afternoon heat, and the background they provided for his story was like a golden brocade.

"I'll tell you how I came to know the emperor, but you must not ever repeat it. This is not to protect me, but to protect you. I am far from reprisal, and his reign is long over.

8

"All my life, I followed my own nose, and was willing to be poor and scorned, since my father brought me up to believe that agreement between more than two people, no matter how sensible or just, quickly becomes a dangerous form of illusion and is soon bound up with pride and power-seeking. I gave free rein to my inclinations — a great luxury, I admit — in books and articles that I wrote, and was able to do so because I ignored the punishments meted out to those who do not conform. I was always ready to embark upon physical labor — as I have done — having known since my childhood the delight of a good day's work in the fields."

"But it's so hard," the little girl said, and she spoke from experience.

"Of course it's hard, but the harder you work, the better you feel — provided that you have some land, as we do, and can grow a good crop."

She nodded gravely.

"When you work in the sun, in your own field, there are no illusions that destroy precious time, no opinions, no intrigues — only infallible natural laws, and they never betray you . . ."

"And when you're sick?"

"That is no betrayal. God and nature promise mortality, and sickness is the rehearsal." He stopped himself short. Though she was attentive, she was uncomprehending, as perhaps she should have been at her age. So he continued.

"I had a difficult career as those things go. I managed in just a few years to alienate almost everyone in the capital, and yet I turned to no one for aid or protection. As you know, I found the very fact of people in comfortable agreement objectionable. It actually caused me to have the physical feeling that African termites were crawling

11

all over my body, which is the same feeling I get when I have to wear formal dress.

"The older I got, the poorer I became, until I had to live in a small part of the attic of a barn on a turkey farm at the edge of the city. The roof was so low that I could only stand up in the center of the floor, and I was always smashing my face into beams."

"That's terrible!"

"I managed. I had learned to look far beyond oblivion, and I was not disappointed in what I saw."

"I mean about the beams."

"Oh. Just a few bruises, nothing serious. Anyway, one rainy night, as I was trying to work by the light of a turkey-fat lamp — I could hardly see: turkeys are not known for the brilliance of their fat — I heard horses gallop up to the barn. It sounded like a patrol of dragoons.

"I thought it was the tax authorities, come to count the turkeys. They did that, you know, even in the middle of the night. Then they would come into my garret to measure my furniture and weigh my ink bottles. Once, they counted the feathers in my pillow and taxed me on the excess over five hundred, plus interest and penalties for every night that I didn't sleep with an Indonesian dictionary balanced on my chest. 'Why?' I asked. 'You must assume,' they told me, 'that we require everything of you, and that you are free to do only what we specifically exempt. We have exempted all other parts of the body and all other materials from the night-balance requirement. Also, it is your right to substitute for the Indonesian dictionary any five consecutive journals of the Brazilian Anti-Stuttering League. Mind you, if you do so, you must file the appropriate forms as specified in our bulletins, and you are responsible for keeping the forms updated as their format changes.'

"But that night the sound of boots did not stop in the barn, for turkey counting. Up the stairs it came. There was a knock at my door, a polite knock, almost a French knock. I answered it. A colonel and his subalterns snapped to attention on the landing. Their lantern blinded me. 'What do you want?' I asked in the tiny voice that exists for tax collectors.

" 'The emperor requests that he honor you by allowing you to meet him,' they said.

" 'Me?'

" 'Are you the genius who recently proposed a balloon bridge over the Danube?'

" 'Yes.'

" 'Then you're it.'

" 'What emperor?'

" 'There is only one, sir.'

"When they saw that I was frozen in disbelief and could not have moved by myself, they picked me up by the arms. On our way down the stairs I asked if I should not change into better clothes.

" 'Do you have any?' they asked.

" 'No,' I said, shaking my head.

"We galloped through the capital, rattling windows in coffee houses and putting out street lamps with the sweep of cool air that followed our massive Damavand horses. I had always walked across the city. Now I flew. I wondered what I might have done to offend the emperor — did he detest balloon bridges? — and in so wondering, my sense of strength returned. I would not fear him if he had decided to punish me. I would not fawn on him or try to curry favor if he had chosen to reward me. I would ignore the material trappings that men of high station use to hypnotize those over whom they wield power. In short, I decided to remember where we both stood in the eyes of

13

God, and to be myself rather than some special persona invented to please or defy him.

"At the palace, they took me through ten thousand heavily gilded rooms and corridors lit by fireplaces as big as the gates of a brewery, and candelabra that looked like flaming trees. Orchestras sounded in several directions. I peered out the window of one long hall and saw in a ballroom across a courtyard at least a thousand men and women dancing quadrilles."

"What are quadrilles?"

"I don't know. Whenever I see a large number of people dancing, I assume they are dancing quadrilles.

"Imagine the volume of calculation going on in the minds of those privileged folk as they danced. It must have shamed the counting houses of Bessarabia. And they all were scheming to gain favor in the eyes of those whose eyes had looked upon the emperor himself. Meanwhile, I, in my pantaloons with holes in the knees, was being walked past them right to the man of whom they dreamed. And how did I get myself in such an envied position? I didn't do anything. I merely said what I took to be the truth, with no calculation whatsoever. And I had never had the desire to be in the emperor's good graces, since a man of my profession, unless he has betrayed what has brought him to it in the first place, has no need of favors.

"Now, you would think that the emperor would be some sort of giant in very fancy clothes, sitting on a throne in a high tower somewhere in his labyrinthine palace, surrounded by beautiful young women in coquettish fluster and officers throwing out their chests like combat pigeons. Not at all. They brought me to a white-bearded bald old fellow who was lying on a worn Turkoman carpet in front of a half-dead fire. He had a book beside him, a catalogue of his railroad

14

bridges, and he held a pen between his toes. He used his magnificent, sleepy, burgundy-and-gold-colored hunting dogs — dozens of them, Anatoles, Purgamanians, Zywynies, Bosteroles, and Voolenhausers — as pillows and rugs. Even if he rested his elbow on one's head, it only wrinkled up its eyes and continued its dream of fetching birds from the reeds. It was an odd and tranquil scene. And you could hear strains of a waltz coming from deep within the palace.

" 'Are you the emperor?' I asked, because at first I thought he might be a dog-handler or a groom.

"This seemed to amuse him. It was he: I recognized him from postage stamps.

" 'No wonder you're the emperor,' I said. 'You can write with your foot.'

" 'Not really. I just keep my pen there sometimes,' he answered. 'But wait, maybe I can. What an excellent way to send orders to my foot soldiers. Call for a tablet.'

" 'How?'

" 'Just call.'

" 'Just say *tablet*?'

" 'Yes, my voice is tired.'

" 'I'm not used to giving orders.'

" 'I am. Do it.'

" 'Tablet!' I screamed. The door flew open so quickly that I jumped back in surprise, and a liveried servant appeared with a vellum tablet. While I held it, the emperor tried to write with the pen held in his toes. He didn't do very well. Then he had me try it. I didn't do very well either. Now I breathed a little easier, because I knew we had something in common.

" 'Venison pâté and blackberry juice!' he shouted. The door popped open, and they appeared. We began to eat and drink.

15

"I could no longer ignore his costume. 'Are those pajamas?' I asked.

" 'Of course not! This is military underwear! Today I inspected a regiment of my hussars.'

" 'In underwear?'

" 'Yes, in underwear, with a uniform over it.' He pointed to a uniform hanging on a wooden peg near the fire, and threw a piece of wood into the dying flames.

"Noting the heavy pistol on the belt of his tunic, I asked, 'Do you need a license to carry that?'

" 'Me?'

" 'Yes.'

" 'I don't think so. I think, as far as I know, that *personally* I can do anything I want.'

" 'Can you cross the street against traffic?'

" 'When I'm around, there isn't any. They block off all the roads.'

" 'That means you've never seen vehicular congestion.'

" 'Only from a distance,' he said, and then, with some concern that I might think he had led a protected life (as if he hadn't), he added, 'I've seen lots of troops, though, and lots of birds flying around. Pheasants, you know, when flushed in great numbers, tend to bump and collide. What would you call that?'

" 'I would have great difficulty finding a name for it.'

"And then, as if to change the subject, he said, 'I find this venison pâté a trifle too rich. It appears to be seventy percent truffles, and it should be fifty percent. We must have had a rotation in the corps of pâté chefs.'

" 'I think it's magnificent,' I said. 'Anyway, it's better than turkey feet.'

" 'To me,' he said with a sigh, 'it's like potatoes. I have it all the

16

time. I say it and it appears. It's boring, but how can the populace live without it?'

" 'They've never had it, that's how.'

"After a silence, he asked, 'Have you ever played *le grand choisule?*'

"I shook my head. *Le grand choisule* was the secret imperial card game. He taught me the suits, jests, combos, and fouls, and we played until four o'clock in the morning. Then he screamed 'Cushion!' and some carefully dressed servants rushed in to station a satin-covered down pillow between his head and a dog. As he fell asleep, I was ushered out.

"For the next year and a half, I went to see him at least twice a week. We kept it secret; no one ever knew."

"Why?" the little girl asked. "Weren't you proud to see the emperor?"

"I was neither proud nor ashamed. That's not the point. I hadn't realized to what extent the emperor was surrounded by counselors and high-level sycophants who measured their lives by how much they could influence his decisions or control his schedule. These people, especially one who was called Von Rothbart, were entirely capable of ordering my assassination merely to assure their position at court. Von Rothbart himself would have been capable of ordering my assassination if he had known that I was getting good at *le grand choisule.* He had once had a waiter decapitated because there were no peppercorns in the pepper grinder.

"Because all the power of the state was concentrated in the person of the emperor, even the littlest things — whom he glanced at during dessert, whether he yawned when he spoke to this or that noble, his sudden affection for the color blue — had profound and exaggerated consequences. If his advisers or the nobility had known that I had been advising him, I wouldn't have lasted very long."

19

"You advised him?"

"Certainly. We soon tired of playing cards and talking about pheasants. The emperor knew a thousand things about pheasants. But what then? The conversation quickly turned to other topics — semantics, etymology, agriculture, military strategy, aesthetics, diplomacy, and of course politics — with which I had been familiar all my adult life, devoting myself to them with no thought of gain. He had summoned me in the first place because he had read my articles, especially the one about building a bicycle path across the empire, and he wanted to talk.

"Talk we did, for eighteen months. I witnessed the implementation of some of my ideas — hot-chocolate stations on the road to Innsbruck, various types of land reform, free haircuts for varlets — but not many."

"Why not many?" the child asked. "He was the emperor, and could do anything he wanted."

"*Personally.* In matters of *state*, he was much constrained, not least by Von Rothbart, who was almost a shadow emperor. Von Rothbart controlled several divisions and key garrisons of the army, he had his hand deep in the treasury, and he was director of the secret police. Everyone in the empire was afraid of him. Even his appearance was terrifying. He was taller than any man I have ever seen. He wore black capes and tricornered hats, and he often appeared in domino, which is a mask and hood."

"Why would he want to do that?"

"To frighten peple. To build his power, he ruined many a life and took not a few others."

The child seemed not to understand the simple sentence the old man had just uttered.

"You cannot understand," he said, "that to advance his position and aggrandize himself, a man might harm others — and not merely those with whom he was in competition, but innocents."

"What innocents?" she asked.

At this, the old man turned and looked beyond the lines of golden sheaves spread across the fields. He put his hands up to shield his eyes from the bright sunlight.

"What innocents?" she insisted.

"Must you know?"

Though she gave no answer, the answer was clear in the quality of her silence.

"Yes, you must know," he said, and turned back to her, his face flushed in the strong light. "I well understand that you must know, and I will tell you.

"Just to the east of the capital, over the twin channels of the Danube, is a great lake, which you have never seen. It is wide enough that were you to stand on one bank you would not be able to make out a white horse standing on the other, and it is so long that the fastest inland packet takes ten days to go from one end to the other. It bends gently now and then, running flat and smooth below mountains like ours, their white ice reflecting in its deep waters.

"After ten days on the boat, you alight amid the mountains, where a long valley stretches farther still to the east. This is the valley of the Damavand. Three weeks of hard riding on the valley floor will bring you to the easternmost parts of the empire. There, on high plains bereft of forests and lakes, lives a nation of incomparable horsemen. They, the Damavand, are wedded to their horses and appear to grow out of their saddles. Sometimes you see one of them reading a newspaper while standing on the back of his horse as it runs at full speed and takes high walls or hedgerows.

"Partly because of their inordinate fascination with horses and horsemanship, their province is not economically well developed. But, needless to say, they mount the best cavalry the world has ever seen, and it is they who defend the eastern borders of the empire from the Golden Horde. They need not be but they are intensely loyal, and they have always been allowed to run their own affairs, both from gratitude and from necessity. For you cannot tame them; they are horsemen who are born with a blue horizon in their eyes, and no matter how fast they gallop, that horizon recedes.

"The Damavand princes traced their ancestry to the remarkable men who watched from the ground as the Golden Horde conquered their land and burned their dwellings, and who then bravely and ingeniously took to horseback themselves, surprising their conquerors from the rear and the flank, trapping them against the wall of the mountains, and annihilating them. What did it take for sedentary farmers to mount and suddenly become ravishing cavalry? It took a miracle, and as their joy at exceeding their own expectations spread from troop to troop, it made even the captured nomadic horses happy to go against their former masters.

"Unlike western princes, the Damavand did not live in brittle palaces but in brightly colored tents. They went freely among their subjects and were hard riders. Their wealth was in their horses, their herds, and the great monasteries they endowed. All the emperors, from the very beginning, had treated them with respect. The eastern province had always been fertile, content, and marvelously strong.

"Von Rothbart, however, could not resist making inroads to the east. Unbeknownst to the emperor, he sent brigades of fusiliers and garrisoned them on the plains, he increased taxes little by little, and

he drafted Damavand cavalry to serve in places as remote and inhospitable to them as the West Glaciers and the Baltic herring flats.

"At first the Damavand made no protest, as there was much they would tolerate in their loyalty to the empire. But as the pressures grew, Prince Esterhazy, their sovereign, guessed that they might be suffering without the emperor's consent. He decided to go the capital and petition the emperor directly, and to take with him his wife — who was tall, beautiful, and blonde like her Kazakh forebears — and their daughter, the infant Princess Odette.

"The Damavand princes had always been taught self-reliance and frugality. Because of this, and because he wanted to make good time, Prince Esterhazy dispensed with his retainers and set out for the capital. The infant princess was strapped tightly to her mother's back as her mother and father galloped west on two horses, one white and one gray.

"After they had been on the road for several days and had come to the steep cliffs that form the west wall of the province, they were accosted by a group of bandits in a defile where the road narrows to almost nothing. The bandits stood by the horses and blocked the path, expecting the prince and his wife to wheel and run. A slide of heavy rocks and tree trunks had been readied to trap them in retreat.

"But the prince spurred his horse forward, his wife followed suit, and their heavy mounts rammed the bandits' mountain ponies, sending three of them, and their masters, into a rushing river far below, from which they were never to emerge. As his wife and child pulled ahead, the prince held back, and turned in the saddle.

"While his horse was cantering smoothly along the road, he calmly removed from his quiver a short and powerful Mongol bow. The bandits had firearms, and as they gained on him they fired wildly. But

25

only when they were within range did he draw the bow and loose his first shot. An arrow of lignum vitae and steel penetrated the breast of one of the bandits with the sound of a cleaver spliting an apple, and neatly removed him from the saddle. This action was so smooth and quick that the other bandits hadn't time to know it for what it was, and they still thought the prince had his back to them. They continued on. When they fired, he did not flinch, for flinching would have done him no good. Instead, he drew his bow for a second time. The bow's short length hardly showed, but the second arrow, heavy and straight, flew through the air and felled one of the four remaining bandits as if he had collided with an oak limb hanging over the road. One second he was on his horse, and less than a second later he wasn't. Suddenly the others brought their horses to a halt.

"The farther west Prince Esterhazy, his wife, and the child sailed on the lake steamer, the more foreign and outlandish they seemed in their seminomadic costume. As horsemen and foresters debarked at easterly ports, they took with them the ways of the Damavand and were replaced by farmers who lived in chalets in well-ordered fields, and then by merchants and professionals returning from vacation cottages with white fences, beds of geraniums, and stone terraces abutting the water. City dwellers in carefully tailored suits, patent boots, and steel-rimmed spectacles stared at the prince as if he had put on his clothes that morning solely for the purpose of offending them.

"Two heads taller than any of the onlookers, the prince filled them with awe, apprehension, and contempt, for they had been raised to 'see and be seen,' whereas he and his wife were riders of horses and interpreters of clouds. He didn't notice the stares and comments, some of them quite nasty. This was to prove his undoing. In capital cities you must take account of gossip and fashion as if they were arrows flying at you. The minor cruelties uttered at dinner parties and in cafés are endowed with a power out of all proportion, but the prince from the far province would not have understood the pettiness of the ruling circle even had he been aware of it. After all, in the Damavand the horizon was synonymous with the curve of the earth, and both were always in sight.

"He did not go immediately to see the emperor. After two weeks' travel, he wanted to rest, and he and his wife found accommodation at a modest inn. They spent days walking the boulevards, amazed that horses pulled enormous wheeled boxes in which people read books and newspapers and drank tiny cups of chocolate, coffee, and tea. In the Damavand, tea was served in a glass. In the capital, they drank from nothing larger than thimbles.

"The little princess was delighted by the animals in the zoo. Though she was completely used to horses, she had never seen a rhinoceros or a giraffe, both of which she found infinitely fascinating because she thought they were horses that had failed to measure up.

"Her parents carefully placed her on the diminutive rides in the children's park. At an archery booth, the prince gathered every prize but one, a rubber artichoke, because he did not understand what it was. They even took the baby to the opera. This was unheard of, and elicited rude stares. But what did they care? They had never heard of opera. They liked it, though, for it reminded them of the open plains they knew so well, even though it transpired in a room with a ceiling. This they thought a miracle worthy of further investigation.

"But they paid dearly for these enjoyable days. Von Rothbart's agents were everywhere and could not help but note so outlandish a family. Their reports languished for a week in a pigeonhole at the headquarters of the secret police, but finally made their way through the bureaucracy until a middle-level official recognized them for what they were. Von Rothbart was delighted. He knew the prince had not seen the emperor, for he knew exactly whom the emperor saw (that is, except for me), and he sent a little spy in a black cape with crimson lining — the man looked like a bat — to the inn, deep in a pine grove, where the prince and his family were staying. The spy confirmed the reports.

"Over a period of several days, Von Rothbart sent five bowmen, each disguised as a traveler, to the inn. These 'salesmen' and 'solicitors' took up positions in rooms facing an inner courtyard. There they waited, peering through the cracks in the shutters. One evening at dusk, the prince and his wife, who carried Princess Odette in her arms, returned from the center of the city and began to walk across the courtyard to their rooms.

"As the lead bowman flung open his shutters, the others followed suit. When the prince heard this, he looked up with great apprehension and saw the archers in the windows, their bows drawn. Before he could put his arms around his wife and daughter, the arrows were released, and each found its way with terrible precision.

"The prince himself was struck by three arrows, and his wife was pierced by two others. They fell, and as soon as they hit the flagstones another volley arrived, doubling their wounds, and then, when they were immobile, another, and then, even after they were dead, another, as fast as the bowmen could set and let fly their arrows.

"Though the prince had thrown himself over his wife too late, she had shielded the child. They died not so much in physical pain as with the far greater anguish of not knowing the fate of their daughter. The child herself was too shocked to cry out, and lay crushed

beneath her mother, covered with blood, in a state that I, for all the things I have seen, cannot imagine.

"The assassins fled, not for fear of being caught but because even they had to flee from the horror of what they had done. They had been instructed to kill the child too, and when their hail of arrows brought complete silence to the little courtyard, they thought they had, because babies cry. They reported to Von Rothbart that he would not be harried by an avenging heir.

"Despite what Von Rothbart thought, the child was alive and unhurt. As soon as the assassins fled, a scullery maid who had witnessed the murders, with no idea whatsoever of why they had occurred, rushed to lift the baby from underneath her mother and father. The maid left on the instant, with the baby in her arms. She did not stop for a moment, and traveled all night on the forest road and for many days thereafter, never returning to the capital. The infant Princess Odette, whose name and a crown were embroidered on her gown, did not cry that terrible night, or any night thereafter, for all her tears had been taken from her."

"Rumors spread through the capital, and whether by hope or by some lively quality of the truth people said that the child of the murdered couple had been spared and had been taken into the forest.

"Day after day, Von Rothbart sent waves of soldiers to search the countryside. Patrols searched every barn within ten days' travel of the Josefstädterstrasse. They searched the immense forest, its lakes, gorges, and stands of giant trees. They discovered an almost infinite number of compassionate hiding places. Once, the woman and child heard horsemen riding through a meadow. They listened as the grasses rustled and broke and the horses snorted, and they retreated into the shadows of a thick glade of trees. The horsemen passed by.

"To excuse their failure in hunting down the child, the soldiers said that her nurse had turned her into a white swan. This was readily believed in the capital not so much because people thought it was true but because they held out hope for her, and her transformation into so graceful a creature seemed both beautiful and just. Still, Von Rothbart would have kept his soldiers out for months, had not everything been eclipsed by the death of the emperor.

"The emperor was an old man, and yet everyone was shocked when he died, for emperors are supposed to be as imperturbable as the state they embody. He was playing chess with the empress when suddenly he threw his arm across the board, upsetting all the pieces, as if he were reaching for a ledge to stop a fall. Though his last words were reported to have been 'Let whosoever comes after me govern wisely and with self-sacrificing justice,' he said in fact, 'Apologize to my pheasants!' No one knew whether he was remorseful or believed the empress had somehow slighted the inhabitants of his hunting preserves. It didn't make any difference. For him, it was all over.

"In the convulsion that followed, Von Rothbart forgot about Princess Odette. As the spring ice broke up on every lake in the empire, he spent his energies in desperate maneuver, and after months of politicking, bribery, and violence, succeeded in making himself regent for the emperor's newborn son, a royal prince who was the first male child in the kindly emperor's forty years of fathering. Though dozens of the emperor's children were scattered over the continent, some already wise and middle-aged, the heir to the throne was a little cross-eyed baby not much bigger than a bullfrog. Von Rothbart, as he saw it, had eighteen or twenty years to make fast his hold on the empire.

"But the emperor had not been a fool. He knew that Von Rothbart would have twenty years' sway, and would watch the boy's development with deep interest. So, to allay Von Rothbart's suspicions, he chose a tutor with no political allies and no support from any faction. He instructed the tutor to appear publicly to be a bumbling and impotent scholar, ignorant of power politics and obsessed with the arcane debates of cosmology and taxonomy; to teach the prince the fundamentals, with an eye to creating within him not only compassion but courage; to make sure that the prince was secretly tutored in combat; and, finally, to wait until the right moment and then entrust the prince with the task of overturning Von Rothbart or whoever had succeeded him. He added, in a letter setting out the requirements, that the tutor should appear to be fond of drink, for Von Rothbart would be delighted to see the prince's teacher crippled by the ceaseless consumption of alcohol."

"How do you know this?" the girl asked, sweeping back a lock of hair. "How could you possibly know?"

"I was the tutor."

"Ah!" the child exclaimed.

"Ah, indeed! I had to pretend to be an alcoholic, which was difficult for me, since my stomach refuses alcohol in any form. I took lessons from a Hungarian actor, and soon was able to appear perpetually intoxicated. I became so good at this that sometimes I had difficulty getting sober.

"Von Rothbart had never heard of me, and did not know of my association with the emperor. In the half-dozen interviews he commanded, I exhibited a great passion for frogs. When he asked me about politics, I told him about the digestive system of frogs. I

33

offered to tutor him in this infinitely fascinating branch of the sciences, and though he seemed extremely pleased, he politely declined. He seemed delighted also by the fact that I stammered in his presence, laughed weakly for no reason, and contrived never to look him in the eye. These humiliations allowed me twenty years to raise a young man upon whom the hope of the empire could rest.

"You would have liked him, I know, as a boy, and as a young man. I had to make him immediately aware of the sadness and tragedy in the world, for failing that, he would not have been able to develop the latent powers that promised, very quietly, to make him an emperor in his own right. He was a serious child most of the time, somewhat like you. I think I did well by him, though he had to be brought up, unlike most princes, with a broken heart."

"The young prince was nearly an orphan. Of course, he had every material advantage, and he even slept in a gold cradle. But, uninfected with the stupidity of their elders, infants can neither crave nor value things like that. In fact, Princess Odette, raised at the same time with only pine boughs for a roof, was probably better off than he, with his nursery the size of a great railway station."

"What about his mother, the queen?"

"The empress."

"The empress, then."

"She was the daughter of minor nobility in the Tyrol. They were what you find *underneath* the bottom of the barrel. They dressed up their daughter to catch the eye of someone in the capital who could support them, and succeeded beyond their wildest expectations, for when the emperor's first wife died he was so confused that he fastened upon the bottom-of-the-barrel girl as if she were heaven itself. She was beautiful, that I will admit, but her interests were confined to dresses, jewelry, and the flattery of half a hundred attendants. During the time she was with child she was so ashamed of her appearance that she fled to the upper storeys of the palace and was not seen in public. And after the prince was born, she gave him over to a wet nurse and took the court to Bogdelice-by-the-Sea.

"She ordered that he be dressed well, and saw him mainly on ceremonial occasions. The rest was left to the staff. Before the emperor had been in his grave two weeks, she began to have affairs, and do you know with whom she formed the most lasting liaison, merely because he was able to flatter her most falsely and procure for her the rarest jewels?"

"Who?"

"Guess."

"No!"

"Yes. Von Rothbart. I had quite a task. The boy had no father, and, in a sense, no mother. I had to keep him undamaged by Von Rothbart, make him strong, and prepare him to take by force the empire to which he was heir.

"The saddest and hardest thing was that I could not let him love me like a father, which meant that I could not appear to love him, as I did, like a son. Whenever we approached such a point — if, for example, he was playing and he reached out to embrace me — I had to draw away."

"But why?" the child asked, since he had not raised her that way.

"Perhaps mistakenly, I believed I had to save a great place in his heart for the father he had never known. Taking on Von Rothbart and his allies would be something the prince would have to do for his own blood, to please a father who could never be pleased. Since I myself did not need an empire salvaged, I would not have been sufficient to fill that place.

"I did succeed in bringing up a serious and troubled young man, which was my aim, since wisdom comes not from fair weather but from storms. And by the time he was eighteen, he was competent in half a dozen languages, the classics, mathematics, and military strategy. He had, of course, studied the history of kingdoms and empires.

"From the time he was little, I had taken him out into the countryside. No one missed him. His mother was too involved with the life of the court to know that we had gone on foot toward Klagenfurt, just the two of us, with me dressed in my pants with holes in the knees, and him in his roughest play clothes. We were on the road for several months of the year, mainly when the weather was good and everyone had gone to the summer palace. Because of this, he understood ordinary people, and was neither gullible nor imperious. He knew he was not to say who he was. It didn't matter; no one would have believed him anyway.

"Once, we camped by a river with boys who were the sons of merchants in Immelstädt and had run away to hunt and climb. For three weeks they were lost in their own society, the prince with them, an equal. They reached the summits of several nearby peaks, they swam in the river and set up a rope off which they flew into a deep pool, and they hunted, although he was profoundly troubled by the killing of helpless animals. It was hard for me to take him back home. He preferred their kind of life to his own. But he had no choice.

"When he was older, I set up a camp in the forest, where we went in the greatest secrecy for military training. I brought in swordsmen, cavalry riders, and archers from the Damavand, which by that time had already rebelled against the empire. Here were the finest soldiers of their kind, practiced in combat against troops fighting under the name of the prince, risking their lives to train him as best they could.

"Von Rothbart and the empress were under the impression that the prince was physically incapable of wielding anything heavier than a plume. We deliberately kept away from sports. He neither hunted nor rode, and had no fencing master. Do you understand how that looked? Even the dairymaids had fencing masters. They thought the prince had been cut off at the knees, which pleased Von Rothbart immensely. But he wouldn't have been pleased had he seen the prince, tutored intensively from the age of four, with a bow, on a horse, or exercising with a saber. No saber master had his strength or alacrity, no cavalryman could turn as well in the saddle or fight with a sword while hanging under his horse. And with his heavy bow the prince could shoot the pips off apples across the Danube so quickly that you would have thought three archers were at work much closer to the targets.

"Boys in late adolescence, even if they are not royal princes, even if they do not excel in marksmanship and other such things, can get astoundingly smug. And why not? They are in the peak of health. Nature itself makes them want to sing and dance. And, in the main, they do not know grievous loss.

"Had he been just anyone, this kind of natural arrogance would have served to power him through the difficult years of his twenties. But he had extraordinary responsibilities. I had to season him, and did so by making him face before he had to the great and insoluble questions that come to us in the normal course of a lifetime, both in suffering and in understanding.

"I confronted him by example (for we had the resources to seek such examples, and it was the right time in history) with death and dying — two different things entirely — with the suffering of children, the slaughter of innocents, and those things of similar gravity that perplex and hurt me not less, but more, as I grow old.

"At first, as I had expected, he gave me facile answers. And just as I had had to withdraw when, as a child, he had come to me with open arms, now I took from him his youth and substituted for it only sadness, confusion, and bitterness. I disillusioned him.

"This was just before his coming of age, an occasion that I knew would be dear to the empress, for then she could gorge herself on ceremony and force him to choose a wife who would resemble her. I also knew that with the prince's coming of age Von Rothbart, now quite old, just as fierce, and triply dangerous, would take certain measures even though he thought the young man was effeminate.

"The empress and Von Rothbart wondered why the prince was so melancholy. Though he did all he was supposed to do — he went to the balls and feasts, and he danced — he was melancholy, and he could not hide it."

"When the prince came of age they had a series of damnable parties and pageants which were no good to anyone except bakers, florists, and the poets and composers commissioned to write odes. Before I was transported from my loft on the turkey farm to my quarters in the royal palace, I had been commissioned to write odes for the declining nobility — *Ode on the Birthday of Baron Stumpf, Ode to the Daughter of Principessa Tantoweeni, Ode on the Restoration of the Pergola at the Country Seat of the Duchess of Tookisheim.* I called them odes,

all right. I always said 'Ode damn' when I had to write one. You break your head for two weeks, and they pay you enough to take a spider to lunch."

The little girl was delighted by this professional complaint, for it suggested that the world was full indeed if the farmer she had known for as long as she could remember could have led at one time so different a life. "What about your quarters in the palace?" she asked. "Were they as big as our house, or bigger?" She was referring to a good cedar cabin, with inimitable views, that was big enough only for the two of them and Anna, with whom she did not want to go down to the plain.

"Really!" he answered. "We are talking about the greatest palace that has ever been built. When I lived in it, it had some seventeen thousand five hundred rooms, a few of which could comfortably hold ten thousand people as they walked around dressed in absurd balloon-like clothing. Eight cavernous halls were used just for storing the keys to the scores of thousands of doors. I knew an old fellow whose title was Cartographer of the Palace and whose job was to teach palace geography to teachers who would then teach servants, mechanics, and the royal family itself.

"To get a message from one part of the palace to another, you put it in a small box and sent it by dumbwaiter to express riders on the roof. They had a system of roads and bridges up there that took four days to cover. Inside, running unseen through the entire structure, were vast service corridors through which traveled horse-drawn wagons laden with firewood, candles, ashes, linens, and flowers.

"The river Von Blimpen diverted into the northern end of the palace and exited in the south. You could row a boat down the tunnel, near the top floor, from which water was drawn into boilers, tubs, fountains, pools, and sinks.

41

"There were indoor hunting preserves, huge tanks for staging mock naval battles, hospitals for hunting birds, grouse-plucking galleries, and pheasant egg incubators. Once, I was surprised to stumble upon a training academy for truffle-sniffing pigs. Each pig had a groom and two handlers, and lived in a big bedroom with *trompe l'oeil* depictions of an oak forest. The classrooms and auditoriums of this academy were tucked into the asparagus storage section of the green spring vegetable kitchens.

"My quarters were perfectly compatible with all this. I had ten bedrooms. What could I do with ten bedrooms? I had twenty bathrooms. One of the bathrooms had its own bathroom, and one had a bathtub so big that it had been used to keep a blue whale that had been trucked from Gibraltar in a giant brine wagon. The library was another thing — five million volumes and two hundred librarians. I had dozens of aides: chefs, tailors, footmen, boatmen, huntsmen, puntsmen, and even acrobats, whom I used to illustrate to the prince the laws of gravity and motion.

"Needless to say, this was too rich an atmosphere for real study, and I used to take him out into the garden, where we would sit on a step and do lessons. In winter we would set up a lamp and work at a heavy wooden table in the idled strawberry kitchens.

"I quickly understood why the emperor had lived in a small room with a worn Turkoman carpet. One of the grandeurs of human beings is that they tire of grandeur. Yes, I like quail eggs on occasion. But eight hundred pounds a day?

"Anyway, when the prince came of age they had an exhausting series of expensive parties. I detest parties. Because of the action on all sides, you must be alert and are constantly distracted. Everything is broken up into the smallest and most inconsequential bits, for which

the only integrative antidote is alcohol, of which I, for medical reasons, cannot partake. And besides, I do not want to hear about the wonderful swimming party at the Duchess of Tookisheim's river palace, thank you very much. And I do not want to talk to the Marquis of Steubenplotz about how he lost his teeth on grapeshot in the ostriches he killed, while all the time he is looking across the room for a glimpse of the empress, as if he were a railroad signalman peering into a tunnel from which he feared might explode the express to Saarbrücken. These affairs were insufferable, and at every odd one I was obliged to play drunk. I sacrificed for my prince, and he knew it.

"At the last of these before the great extravaganza at which he was to choose a wife, he was doing his best to be charming. You see, he was not the smooth youth that he was supposed to have been. He had great difficulty being polite to people whom he really wanted to pick up and swing over his head. When he was not smiling, his eyes were too deep and his face too weathered and wise to be the face of an ineffectual boy. I believe this unsettled Von Rothbart, who didn't know what to make of it.

"The empress appeared, and the prince went through the motions of respect, though he hardly knew her. When he and I looked at her we always saw Von Rothbart's tricornered hat bobbing behind her head, like a bumblebee. Ostensibly she had come to inform the prince that at the next ball he would be surveying princesses, to choose one for eternity, or at least that small part of it in which we imagine that we know what transpires. In this she took great pleasure and he none at all. Everyone knew the schedule. She just wanted to drive it in.

"When she left, the prince could not conceal his unhappiness. To cheer him up, one of the courtiers proposed that we all go hunting. As the sun was due to rise in an hour, this suggestion was enthusiastically received, because the animals would be careless and dreamlike at dawn, and the hunters would have an easy time shooting them. The prince did not want to waste his time, but they virtually carried him away.

"I was old enough to escape such obligations, and I did not go, but much later, upon his return, my pupil told me a wonderful story with which, although he did not realize it, I was already partially familiar.

"Half the joy of hunting is to ride with a hundred horsemen, weapons at your side, thundering over wooden bridges over thundering streams. I do not know the other half. The hunt is only an excuse to form an army and exercise at war, and is one of those things treasured mainly in remembrance. The violent motion of a war horse on the run becomes in immediate recollection as smooth as a waltz. How the peaks and valleys of the gallop are beaten into silky waves I do not know, except that memory is the greatest poet.

"If the prince rode at the head of his courtiers and soldiers on such an expedition, he had to discipline himself and his mount not to pull ahead, because he was supposed to be scared of horses. No one dared pass him until he waved them on, and he did wave them on, quite early. As they overtook him, all agreed to go right when they reached the fork in the forest road, for to the right were the glades in which ran fierce wild boar, and the soldiers were not as fond of hunting birds as they were of mortal combat with the squat berry-eating pigs that could bite off a man's leg as if it were a celery stalk.

"When the prince, now alone, reached the fork in the road, he went left. Veering from the main body enabled him to ride as fast as he wanted to ride, to appear — according to my instructions — fearful of the clash with the boar, to find truly deserted and forgotten country, and merely to watch the birds and deer that, in the company of others, he would have been expected to kill.

48

"He had no desire to kill animals. This was owing not so much to compassion as to respect, for not even memory can conspire to make a smoother line than the track of a bird wheeling silently in the sunshine over blue water. And when deer step gingerly in the heather, their precision of motion is art, and that is not to mention the perfect rocketry of their escapes. Were they to go faster, the result would not be so pleasing, and were they to go slower, they would not appear to be nobly disciplining themselves against flight.

"The prince rode hard for several hours. When he dismounted, he had come to the shore of a vast lake teeming with emerald-and-gray ducks, white swans, and checkered loons. He rested his horse and began to climb a granite cliff that rose straight from the lake. Up he went, past sinewy pines in the cracks, and steplike ledges as smooth and narrow as balcony rails, hanging perilously over the sparkling water, until he reached the top — a dry, lichen-covered floor that seemed to overlook the whole world. A ridge led south to uncharted mountains, but though he looked for a long while at their high and alluring meadows, he turned finally to the lake.

"The lake was a blue jewel that had been broken by the sunlight into infinitely sequined brass. He had to shield his eyes because its surface had become a hundred million little flares. Though the light hurt him, he could not turn away from what he saw. Thousands of cloud-white swans were rising on a column of blue air. They made a rotating pillar that stood on the fire of the lake, and, hardly moving their wide wings, they ascended the morning air in a gorgeous spiral at the top of which was nothing less than the sun itself.

"Whether the prince looked up or down, he was assaulted by light too bright to withstand. And yet the movement of the swans, perfectly orchestrated, held him fast until he could no longer bear the pain, and he collapsed onto the warm rock. The sun beat down upon him, and as it climbed higher in the sky, everything became a waltz of red and amber in swirling currents of white light and bright silver flashes.

"By dusk, he was burning like fire, but the evening was cool. First came the pale blue and then a black sky, and then moonlight, and mists that rose in unpredictable vales at the lake's edge. He did not know if he were awake or dreaming, but when he opened his eyes and looked down upon the lake, it seemed not so distant. It was as though the water had risen, or he could see magically far.

"As if to echo in their motion the roundness of the moon that bathed them in silver light, the swans were dancing in a ring. Their dance was the perfect union of delirium and control, of purity and abandon, of nature and civilization. How did they put together so gentle a thing with so much power, so powerful a thing with so much grace? It was almost an eastern rite, and yet, they were swans, and yet . . .

"Then he could not believe his eyes, and though he insisted to himself that he was dreaming, the dream was so beautiful that he believed it more than what was real. The swans had become women, and the women had then become swans, until he could not separate them or distinguish between their forms.

"He blinked on purpose. He cleared his throat. What were they that in their silence were so eloquent and in their fragility so strong? He knew that dreams and delirium, like fire, can give warmth and heat but cannot finally be grasped. But he knew as well that what he saw before him was so beautiful that it had to be substantial, for imagination could not have been so fine. And though he had been brought beyond his understanding, he refused not to credit his dream with all the depth of the world.

50

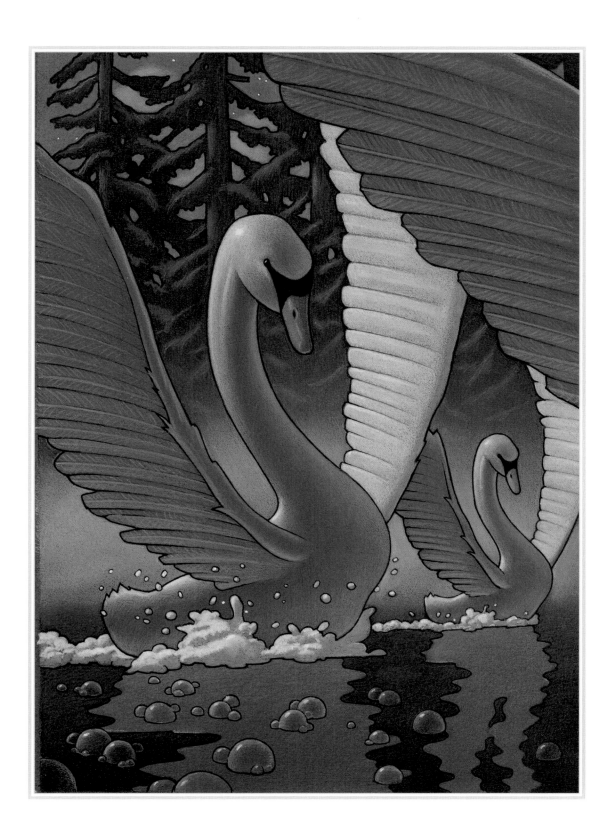

"Then he awakened. He was not in the palace, but still in the forest, though he could tell by the cry of the loons that he was no longer on the ledge. He was inside a little hut. He could hardly see. The only light came from a mass of coals in a small mountain stove. The bed was made of cedar, the blankets homespun.

" 'Where is my horse?' he asked a beautiful young woman who was standing near the door.

" 'Outside,' she said.

"As the days passed and the prince recovered, he watched her from his bed. At first he was taken with her physical beauty, and then with her grace. But he knew that he loved her only after he watched her hands as she sewed, and her eyes following her hands. Only when she concentrated on a task outside herself did he apprehend her real beauty, and when he did, he knew real love for the first time.

"You know who she was, though she herself did not, except for her name, and neither, therefore, could he. She was Odette, and she was the one who, in his dream, had led the swan-maidens in their dance. For this he had a simple explanation. He had seen her when she brought him in, which is why he knew her face, and since the last thing he had remembered had been the swans, he had merely combined the two images. It all made sense — but for the fact that she hadn't brought him in; her companion had.

"When he returned to the city, he told me very little about his stay with her. 'Where have you been?' I asked.

" 'By the shore of a lake, with a woman,' was all he would say.

" 'Who?'

"He shrugged his shoulders.

" 'A milkmaid? Another milkmaid?'

" 'No.'

" 'Who, then?'

"He looked at me blankly.

" 'At least,' I said, 'tell me what she looked like.'

" 'I can't,' he answered. 'You yourself told me that only a painter can describe a face, and then not even he. Faces, you said, are magical. They have not ten features, or twenty, or even two hundred, but thousands, millions, and no deliberate way exists of assessing them.'

" 'But they are appraised easily and immediately in one's heart. I told you that, too.'

" 'Yes, you did.'

" 'And what appraisal did your heart give?'

" 'It told me, from the very first, and then, as each day passed, it told me more and more, that I love her.'

" 'She is a commoner?' I asked. Of course I had nothing against commoners, being one myself, but when a prince falls in love with a commoner, many problems arise.

" 'I don't know,' he said.

Because the prince had been gone for several weeks, all ceremonies had been postponed. Von Rothbart was convinced that the prince was raising an army against him. The foreign princesses at court waited nervously, and they ate so much that they could hardly fit into their fancy dresses.

"When the prince returned, his mother was so enraged that to calm her he told her where he had been. I would have stopped him. But perhaps Von Rothbart would have found him out anyway, either from the love in the prince's eyes, or because he might have been able to recognize the signs of grievance transforming into justice.

"For the second time, Von Rothbart's troops took to the roads in search of Odette. But after his initial indiscretion the prince was quick enough to sense that he had made a mistake, and quick enough still to insist that he had turned on the forest road in the track of the soldiers and courtiers, and, like them, gone off to the right."

"When the prince returned to Odette," the child asked, "did they follow him? I so hope they did not!"

"Things are far more complicated than that," the old man asserted.

"How do you mean?"

"The prince did not go to Odette."

"But he loved her."

"He did. He had come to love her immediately, and she him, which is understandable in view of the circumstances."

"Then why didn't he go to her?"

"He was just old enough to be held by webs of obligation and doubt."

"Webs?"

"For want of a better word."

"I know of no such webs," she said derisively.

"I realize that," the old man answered. "But I do not know how to convey to you how the spirit of a child gradually becomes caged."

She was indignant.

"Don't be upset," he counseled. "One of the great tests in life is to escape that cage while not destroying it. Remaining within it is not inevitable. But you needn't concern yourself with this yet — you're not even ten years old."

He resumed his narrative. "The world of the court and the embassies is more intriguing than you can imagine. Its pleasures sparkle no less for being based entirely on power and privilege, and though they are corrupt, they are hard to refuse. How can I explain them to you?

"On a very superficial level, let us assume that man lives in two worlds: one of God and nature, and the other of his own making. To live entirely in the first and to be satisfied therein is perfectly adequate. Indeed, it is a kind of paradise, which the animals know better than anyone, and without resort to it in some fashion man is nothing more than a machine of his own design. But whereas to live entirely in the world of man is intolerable, to live entirely without it is in some senses equally so. It must be fun to be a squirrel, but think of music, and mathematics, and chocolate cake! The world of man may be imperfection built upon imperfection, but that is what makes it so beguiling — all the accidents and missteps. By the way, do you know why people laugh and animals don't?"

"No," she said, trying to remember if she had ever seen an animal laugh.

"Because people live in a crooked and imperfect place, full of inconsistencies and contradictions. Animals don't laugh because they don't need to: nature is perfect. We have to laugh when we look upon what we have made and what has come of our finely calculated ambitions. Laughter saves us by reconciling our pride to what we really are. Animals — except for cats — have no such need.

"Somtimes, up here where time passes smoothly and slowly, where my own heart, though long broken, is somehow always full, I miss the world below.

"Well, the world of the embassies was self-delighting. Every detail was meant to provide a feeling of walking on air. The women, if not beautiful, contrived to be stunning in appearance, and the artifice they employed had undeniable effect. Powders, perfumes, lotions, dyes, jewels, girdles, pads, and richly colored clothing in combination with a trained bearing can work miracles. For those who were comely to start, the result was breathtaking.

"The food in this world, and I am no lover of any but simple food, had a certain magic. I can't explain it, but the finest food, expertly prepared and served, heightened every word of conversation spoken over it. I cannot comment on the wine, never having been able to drink it. I have mentioned the palace itself. Its fires, flowers, and crystal in great profusion on vast indoor plains of marble and parquet had their own lively effect.

"But none of these things compared with the music. The music was a formula for the most admirable and virtuous intoxication. How they did it — all those musicians, composers, and gypsies — is beyond my understanding, but their music lifted you off the floor and held you effortlessly suspended, lighter than air. For my generation and for those immediately preceding and following, it was the closest approximation we could imagine to the flawless and joyful speech of God.

"The prince was held in place not merely by webs of obligation but by his desire for the world of the court and embassies, for they had a certain shining, not unlike the sunlit glitter of the lake."

"The princesses assembled in the greatest hall of the palace, the one in which the Duke of Tookisheim used to fly his glider. The prince could just as easily have met them one by one in a small room in one of his apartments, or taken a quiet walk with them in one of the many gardens. That's how I would have done it. Or, assuming it had to be a collective endeavor, I would have had them all working with the prince in stacking firewood or baking a nut log. The best way to know someone is by watching him work or struggle, for then he forgets himself and his qualities either shine through or stay dark.

"But no, the procedure was determined by the empress and Von Rothbart. That meant forty thousand pounds of petits fours and thirty thousand magnums of champagne. All the energies of the empire, of herdsmen in the east, fishermen in the north, foresters in the west, and farmers in the south, the accumulated production of the factories and ateliers, the duty of the soldiers, and the genius of the architects and composers, were distilled into a tiny golden droplet. But it was entrancing. You didn't have to approve of it to admit that it was entrancing.

"Thousands and thousands of overdressed people packed the glider hall. So much perfume was in the air that the palace bees, imprisoned in a far wing, broke loose from their confinements and came through the ventilation system to crisscross ecstatically above the dancers, reflecting the bright gas lamps as if they were golden confetti.

"From the gilded bases of these lamps emerged flames as tall as grenadiers, undulating with the music as if they too were dancing. The orchestra was so tremendous that it overflowed the galleries, and so that he could be seen by all his musicians, little Maestro Nahaag, the conductor, had to stand in a lighted crystal booth suspended from the ceiling by chains. Because the empress thought chains were unsightly, she had had them encrusted with pearls. The waiters looked like generals, and the generals were as colorful as Easter eggs: they were plastered so heavily with medals, tassels, and braid that all you could see of them were two little eyes peeping from a breastwork of lapels, like chipmunks in a stone wall. From within their tunics came brave and muffled descriptions of ancient battles.

"The young prince sat on his father's throne, uncomfortably buttoned up in a red jacket with too much gold braid. Nonetheless, he leaned quite comfortably toward the five princesses. They did look beautiful. And that is not only because they had taken four days to dress, but because they *were* beautiful — except for one, who, although quite homely, was the most charming of the lot.

"After they were presented to him, he danced with them one by one, and as they danced they spoke. Because I noticed their powerful effect, I called him over and told him that Odette was also a princess, though she did not know her origins, and that unlike her competitors, she was in a state of undiscovered grace.

"But one princess after another courted him, Von Rothbart pressed champagne upon him, and the music made him giddy, as did being compacted in the clouds of perfumed silk that surrounded his dancing partners. Propelled by the magic of her czardas, the Hungarian seemed to be invading his heart, which is not to say that the Russian, the Circassian, the Pole, and the girl from Naples, with their bell-like voices, were not succeeding too.

"Five hours passed, violin strings began to snap, and waiters fainted under trays of caviar and lobster tails. But the celebrants, the cream of the aristocracy, were just getting started. Waltzing around on floors covered with five inches of diamond-hard wax, shoveling down huge loads of highly expensive food, and sitting immobile for many exhausting hours while fat women trilled at them in foreign languages was their profession. People like that get up at seven in the evening, and at a social function the frailest among them, the nonagenarian earls who would not be able to snap a chicken bone to save their lives, or the obese hippocene duchesses who gasp for every breath as if they have swallowed their ropes of pearls, can outlast the greatest athletes who have ever lived.

"I was falling off my feet, pretending to have taken too much champagne, ready to faint from fatigue and discouragement. I had lost all opportunity to influence the prince. He hadn't always listened to me, but now I couldn't even get near him.

"Then the grand waltz began. Ten thousand couples circulated in billowy waves, turning slowly, their forward momentum like that of a wind-driven tide. As beautiful as it was, it still reminded me of bumper cars in the Tivoli. Every now and then I saw the prince floating by, enwrapt in the arms of a magnificent woman.

"At the very peak of the delirium, Von Rothbart jumped up on a marble pedestal, drew a pistol, and fired it in the air. All I could do was watch and regret as a way opened in the hall, and between two ranks of startled aristocrats came the most physically beautiful woman I had ever seen. She was dressed in black, as if to say, 'Judge me by myself alone.' Even now I am unsettled when I think of the perfection and voluptuousness of her features. In her walk across the floor, she seized every eye. The timing of her steps was as rhythmic and even as a dance. She was so graceful that no one would have been surprised had she sailed on the wind and turned as smoothly as a bird.

"Although I didn't know it then, she looked much like Odette, but whereas Odette was open and innocent, she was as tight as a jewel. Even her name was similar. I winced when Von Rothbart introduced her as Odile.

"In the middle of what had become a hall of pounding hearts, the prince stepped forward, forgetting himself, forgetting all others, forgetting Odette, and held out his arms to take Odile in a dance. When his hand touched hers, it was almost as if we in the hall were ourselves overwhelmed in a real embrace. And when he began to dance with her and their bodies touched, even I, in the depth of defeat, felt pleasure.

"Von Rothbart signaled the conductor, who began a waltz so smooth and hypnotic that it bullied time and banished gravity. A huge sea

opened among the dancers. From the sidelines, stunned and delighted guests, and older people who should have been wiser, watched transfixed as the prince and Odile slowly turned across the floor.

"That night he chose her as his bride, and in so doing he chose the world of the court and the embassies over the world of the forest and the lakes."

Hearing this, the child wanted to cry. The old man, however, knew that most stories never really end but, rather, take on a new form, and he continued. "I could think only of Odette," he said. "I hadn't told the prince about her history for fear that he would love her from pity. But now it was too late. Once, I had believed that Von Rothbart's archers had had the last word. Then I had hoped it would not be so. Now, though I felt as keenly for Odette as I might have had I been her father, I had no way to help her. I was deeply moved by the thought of Odette waiting in the forest for the prince, not realizing what he had done, never to see him again. But I didn't know the least of it, for I was not aware that she was soon to bear his child."

"Two years passed. The prince forgot the simple things that once he had loved, and spent his waking hours with Odile, his mother, and Von Rothbart, immersed in the pleasures of the court. In his ceaseless occupation with the flow and control of power and riches and his worship of the cold beauty of Odile, he became a stranger to me, and I was left with my books, instruments, and globes, none of which interested him any longer, and none of which, I confess, interested me. Neither, I might add, did Odile. Apart from her stunning proportions, I could not see what the prince saw in her. She was nearly inanimate, like a rock in a display case, or a portrait that has gone wrong because the painter is a painter more of things than of people.

"But for one incident, about a year and a half after his marriage to Odile, I would have thought that the prince had lost his soul. I was sitting on one of our former tutorial benches, under an overhanging eave in a kitchen courtyard. It was raining heavily, as it must in spring to melt the snow so that summer can blaze across the steppes in green and blue. Watching the rain collide at an angle with a brick wall and then run down it in a tight embrace, I was trying to determine why at a certain volume and force the water bounced off, and why, if neither was sufficient, it didn't. I came to the conclusion that the gross mechanics were directly attributable to the molecular structure of the water, and that the thresholds of adhesion were determined by group particle affinity. I believe I was slightly ahead of my time.

"Anyway, I was intently absorbed, speaking to myself in calculations. When next I looked up, the prince was beside me. 'I didn't see you,' I said.

" 'I know,' he replied. 'You've been muttering numbers in a kind of song.'

" 'Forgive me,' I said dryly.

" 'Forgiven,' he said, twice as dryly, for he, after all, was a prince. This hurt me, for in truth I did love him like a son.

" 'What were you doing?' he asked.

" 'Calculating the force of impact between a given amount of water and a porous surface, such as brick, necessary for the deflection of the water rather than its adhesion.'

" 'In what units?'

" 'In cubic armands per centipede.'

" 'How can you do that without instruments?'

" 'How can you do it *with* instruments? Estimates — it's all estimates. Just as you fall in love with a voice or a face: all is most powerful precisely in the absence of precision. And since measurement, no matter how exact, is nothing more than an analogy of unfixable quantities, I am, my prince, unafraid to estimate.'

" 'You are unafraid of anything, Tutor, are you not?'

" 'Not so.'

" 'I thought you were fearless. Come, now. You *are* fearless. I believe that you would look into my eyes and tell me that I am corrupt. You would even go against Von Rothbart, wouldn't you?'

" 'Have you become Von Rothbart's spy?' I asked, amazed at his transformation. 'But, yes, certainly I would. That is not what I fear. I am of an age, and I have had a life, whereby I no longer fear what may become of me. But almost as if in compensation, reciprocally, I fear much more and suffer greatly on behalf of others.'

" 'The world in general?' he asked, as if I had been making a political argument.

" 'You know that I am not like that. Love for all is love for none.'

" 'Who, then?'

" 'Those who are pure,' I replied, and it went right to him, for he knew whom I meant. 'Those who suffer. Those who wait.'

"The silence that followed was interrupted as one of the orchestras began to tune in a nearby hall. I have always regarded a first-class orchestra tuning its instruments as a toy shop for the ear. We listened to trumpets, violins, drums, and woodwinds playing their scales, while all the time watching the rain run down the saturated bricks. Then, almost tentatively, the orchestra began to play short but powerful sections from the most beautiful symphonies.

"The wind and rain picked up until the water crossed the threshold of surface tension and molecular adhesion and began to dash off the wall. I turned to the prince, as in the old days, to remark upon this, and when I did I saw that he was looking straight ahead, and that tears were running down his face."

"Soon it was again alpine summer, that cool season unlike any other. Don't ask me how it can contain the freedom and joy of summer simultaneously with the gravity and depth of winter. Ask the mountains."

"I will," the child said, for the mountains were right there, guardians of beauty, immobility, and peace.

"The prince begged me to go on the hunt. I told him that I had no desire to kill anything but Von Rothbart. This was not the kind of joke you made in those times. He laughed anyway, and asked me again. I told him that I was serious, that there was far too much to eat in the palace to justify hunting. I told him that I regretted the idea. I told him half a dozen other things, too. But I went.

"We left early in the morning, half a hundred of us, on the best horses that could be looted from the Damavand. We thundered over the bridges and raced through the forest alleys, intimidating even the pine boughs, which swayed in the breeze as we passed."

"Weren't you frightened?"

"Of what?"

"Of falling off the horse, of the bows and arrows, of the soldiers?"

"Of course not. I knew how to ride a horse. I had been a soldier once, adept with sword and bow."

"You had?" she asked, delighted.

"Yes. Is that so surprising?"

"When?"

"When I was a young man."

"Then you've done everything, Grandfather."

"Not everything," he said, "not yet.

"That day I rode forth with great regret but not without vigor or skill. The prince had long shed the pretense that he was inept, and though he was merely gliding at his ease, the rest of the troop had difficulty keeping up with him.

"These men — the best soldiers of the empire — were so skilled that they loosed arrows on the gallop, left and right, bringing down the animals that the thunder of the Damavand horses' hoofs had flushed from places of refuge. Sometimes the arrows killed the birds and fawns immediately, and sometimes they just wounded them. As we rode, we left scores of stricken animals to die, having reduced creatures of the greatest beauty and grace to nothing. I had seen such things before, of course, and worse.

"The prince took part. I was sure that if he would so wantonly kill, he was lost. But I rode on.

"We exited from the dark forest and its tall, fragrant trees, exploding into the sunlight. Confused and delighted by the brightness, we halted by a lake to water the horses and to rest.

"The fifty Damavand stallions were in an orderly row, their necks bent to drink, their tails swishing, their silken wet flanks glistening in the light. You don't have to hobble Damavand horses near water. They don't run away or spook with water nearby, because they come from a place that's dry.

"Soldiers, huntsmen, and courtiers reclined on a bank. Some slept in the glaring sun. We were all tired, as we had left early in the morning and had been riding hard.

"I too was about to sleep, when I saw the prince sit up with a start. He jumped to his feet, bow in hand, and stepped forward. Almost as if the number had been predetermined, as many swans as there were hunters sailed like a battle fleet around a near point in the lake. Oblivious of the danger, they made right for us.

"Others now awakened and stood, pulling arrows from their quivers and threading their bows. Soon everyone was up, standing silently on the bank, waiting for the procession of swans. When the swans came within shooting distance, I looked sadly at the prince.

"But he had not pulled his bow. He waited, transfixed, until the swans had come too close for sport. Then he turned and commanded that all in our party hold their arrows.

"To see the swans go by and the arrows stayed was for me a great thing. I saw the prince's face change before my eyes. I believed that he knew then what he loved, whom he loved, and what was to become of him. He was not unhappy, and he must have been comforted by a discovery of great beauty — if you will allow, as I always have, that beauty is what makes us happy even in the knowledge of our certain demise.

"What then hapened was bound to happen. Some of Von Rothbart's lieutenants, trained not to respect the prince — which was partially my fault — could not restrain themselves in the presence of so attractive a target, and disregarded his order. They pulled back their bowstrings. Three arrows traveled low over the water and lodged deep in the breasts of three swans.

"It was as if the prince himself were struck. Even the others, inured to the kill, grimaced at the sight of the swans dying in water reddened with their own blood. They died not only of their wounds, but, thrown off balance by the arrows, they drowned, rolling over without being able to right themselves, their long necks thrust downward.

"The prince's face tightened in an expression I have seen only in battle, and rarely even then. I knew that a violent act was about to occur, and that it was inevitable — as if he were not a man but a wave about to break or lightning about to uncoil from a thundercloud.

"He loaded the first arrow faster than anyone could see and sent it into the heart of the first of Von Rothbart's lieutenants. Before the other could turn, his heart, too, was stopped forever. The third man let off a shot at the prince, who dropped to dodge it. It flew by us invisibly, but we could hear it. In one movement the prince rose, loaded another arrow, and plucked his bowstring. The arrow went straight to its target.

"Now the world had come apart, and the heart of the empire would divide in two, as the emperor had foreseen: Von Rothbart against the prince. Both were able and prepared. None of us standing there had any doubt whatsoever that the war would be long and terrible. In truth, as soldiers and former soldiers, we all expected to die.

"Stunned and immoblile, we remained on the shore of the lake, overtaken by the amazement of having witnessed the separation of one era from another. It was as if highest summer had become darkest winter with the unexpectedness of a thundercrack in the snow.

"In the paralysis and confusion of the moment, the prince, now free, mounted and rode away. Several of Von Rothbart's men went after him. I myself stayed where I was, not knowing quite what to do."

"I hope it was the best ride of his life. I have often thought of what it might have been like, of what he might have been thinking and how he felt. I doubt that he was planning a rebellion. The clarity of those last hours must have allowed him to see that he

73

had little chance of success — not because he wasn't able, but because his interests had turned elsewhere. All the while, when he was imprisoned at court, he had been growing and he had changed. To unseat Von Rothbart, he would have had to become a general, to deal primarily with objective forces — strategy, logistics, and politics. But I am convinced that he had been conquered by the world of the heart and all the possibilities therein. He had seen that some small and seemingly powerless actions, or simple coalitions of light, sound, and color, can be supremely powerful in regard to the soul of a man, and can take him to other worlds. And he had seen that, though sometimes hidden, they exist in this world in legions, in armies, in multitudes. I am sure that when he saw the swans gliding around the point he apprehended another realm, as one sometimes does, and was ready to follow, far into oblivion, wherever it led in darkness or in light.

"With this resolution comes the greatest surge of freedom anyone can know. And if you couple it with an escape on horseback through the pines and meadows of a mountain forest in summer, with clouds moving in slow counterpoint across a field of azure, then perhaps you can imagine what he felt.

"I see the sharp ears of his Damavand horse bobbing in the wind as the roads and trails are rapidly consumed underneath. I see the evergreens flowing by, closing behind the prince and his horse in a wall of dark green like a wake. I feel the wind, the velocity, his sense of flying and rising.

"He may have known that Von Rothbart's men were close behind, for to follow him into the tighter curves and through the deepest part of the forest they would have had to have been close. He may not have cared, or perhaps he was unaware. Had he known what awaited him, I imagine, he would have turned to kill his pursuers.

"When he reached the hut, he did turn to look at them, and they stopped and rode away. Then he went inside. Imagine what he felt upon finding not only Odette but a small child in her arms — his own. And when he dismounted, the child's face lit up. Having a child to protect makes impossible the kind of metaphysics he was contemplating on his ride, the risks and glories and whatever they may require in regard to sacrifice and dying. With a baby to care for, you must be as prudent as a grocer. But he had already thrown down the challenge, and they were as deep in the forest as you can get, with nowhere to flee: other parts of the empire did not have the same kind of sheltering terrain.

"He had one day with the infant and Odette, during which he and Odette must have known what awaited them and their child."

"With a hundred and fifty of his best men, Von Rothbart left the city. Except for the Damavand warriors, weeks away, no formation existed with the power to counter them. The army was scattered in the disintegrating provinces, and spoiled by irregular warfare in fixed positions, its cavalry had long before lost its edge. Even had a force to counter Von Rothbart's existed, I could not have mobilized it fast enough to have caught him. He would have had a considerable head start, and he was not going off to fight a battle, which might have offered delays, but to murder.

"I rode behind them, hoping that I would be able to warn the prince and Odette. But as I hadn't any idea of where the prince and Odette were, I could only follow. I dreamed of riding through Von Rothbart's ranks at the very last, but I knew that I was too old for such things, and that his soldiers would cut me down. I thought of stopping him with a shot from my bow, but I was not the bowman I once had been. Still, I followed relentlessly, with no more control of my forward career than if my horse and I had been falling off a mountainside.

"The soldiers hardly stopped in the clearing before the cabin. Instead, they made a wide turn and increased their speed. They had seen the prince and Odette at the top of a high meadow to the south.

"I wondered why the two of them were not mounted, and why they had gone to such an open place, where they were immediately observed. There, on foot, they had no chance whatsoever.

"This I simply could not understand until just after the soldiers had left the clearing, for then I saw an old woman dart from the cabin, with a baby swaddled in her arms. At first I was confused, but as they disappeared into the forest I understood everything, and I was so moved, and so proud of the young man I had raised, that I could hardly go on.

"But I had to go on. I rode up onto the meadow as fast as I could, so slowly, it seemed, that I wondered if I were dreaming.

"Von Rothbart did not dare approach the prince until his archers had dismounted and drawn their bows. Then he walked his horse ahead and halted. The prince and Odette were on the edge of a bluff so far above the lake that the lake's waves looked like a light coat of oil refracting the sunlight. This must have been where he had seen the swans rise in a gold-and-white column.

"When I arrived, the arms of the bowmen were quivering, their arrows set to fly. I was behind their line, but still close to my boy and Odette. He smiled at me as if to stay any action, as if to say that he was content, and as if to say goodbye. But how could he have been content, except perhaps in knowing that his child had escaped?

"I could do nothing against a hundred and fifty archers with their arrows aimed. The wind that rose from the lake, flowed over the cliff after its dizzying climb, and made Odette's homespun dress luff at her ankles, carried her words to me. This was the first time I had seen her, and the last. She was very beautiful: you should know that. It is important for you to know that. She was in his arms, facing him, and she said, gently, 'I am afaid of nothing, but I cannot abide being killed by arrows.' Without realizing it, she had remembered her mother and her father.

"Then, with the saddest expressions I have ever seen, they looked into one another's eyes, held tight, and leaned into the wind. For a terrible moment we watched them fall, until they disappeared from view. May God forgive me if this is no more than an illusion that I myself have created, but they did not tumble or become entangled, they fell with what appeared to be increasing slowness. They fell as if they knew how to take to the air. They fell in smooth dampened curves that promised flight."

"When Von Rothbart wheeled his horse about in that meadow, he knew the empire was his. Though he would be censured for the death of the prince, he could justify it, and in truth he had not killed him.

"And as far as Von Rothbart knows," the old man said, turning to look the child straight in her eyes, "there are no heirs."

"But there are!" she exclaimed.

"Yes. There is an heir, who may someday return to claim a kingdom and an empire, though I am far from sure that this is what the prince and Odette would have wanted. Nonetheless, it will be up to their child to decide in what realms she will go."

"She?" the child asked, already deeply loyal to the rightful heir.

"She," he repeated.

"How do you know?"

The old man nodded before he spoke. "After the others were gone, I found myself in no condition to move. For an hour or so I remained above the lake, not daring to look down but instead trying to summon in my memory as best I could the image of those two young people. Every death that truly touches you hastens your own, and when it is the death of someone so young — well, for an old man like me, it is almost unbearable.

"I confess that in those moments I thought of joining them, and I suspect that following them would not have been difficult. As I contemplated this, standing near the edge, I heard a whistling in the air, like that of powerful wings. The upwelling of the wind had brought the sound to me early. I dared not look, and I did not have to, for the sound was rising.

"I faulted myself for wishful thinking, and I told myself that even were I not imagining this sound, its significance would lie only in what I wished rather than in what was. There are certain great and beautiful things that to all appearances find defeat in this world. All proof, all reason, show them to have fallen, and as often as not our hope is merely our punishment. But in this world there are as well wrenching and great surprises that take us beyond what we can reason and what we can prove.

"I have merely my hope, but I have it still. I have not abandoned it, and will not. The sound was the sound of wings. They rose, and their whistling and beating on the wind grew so loud that it deafened me. I shuddered before they cleared the edge. They came on with great speed. They did clear the edge, and they filled the sky — two swans, wings extended, riding on the air and powering themselves ahead. They went right over me at great speed and disappeared beyond the

trees as if they had a most specific and compelling destination. And I was left with nothing but the sound of wings echoing in my ears.

"Far away, on the crest of meadows leading into the high mountains, I saw the figure of the woman who had fled from the cabin. Though I would have to descend, and go around the lake, I knew I could reach her before dark, because my horse was a good horse."

The child, whom he loved so much, had begun to cry.

"I have always known, from the way that Odette remembered without memory, that, even without memory, their daughter would dream of finding them, and that she, too, would be loyal. But they are gone, and she cannot find them, except perhaps in the beating of her own heart, or when in the quiet of the forest a swan takes flight, and the white blaze of its wings brings them to life in her eyes."

Now she was sobbing. He took her in his arms and stroked her head. "You needn't grieve," he said, "for the story has come full circle, and you know the end. My horse was a good horse. I was able to reach them, on a high meadow, before dark — the woman and the infant child — and I have remained with them ever since."

BOOK TWO

A CITY
IN WINTER

went down to the city on the plain when I was not yet ten years old, only a short time after I had discovered who I was and whence I had come. My story is simple, the story of struggle, so well known to all who come into this world, and I am writing for you, my son or daughter not yet born, so that you too may know who you are and whence you have come. Listen to the tale, which is also yours, and is told for love. Come back to me, come back to this time before you were born, to a golden morning in December as the sunlight frosts the city roofs, and a thousand singlets of smoke rise to the pure blue heavens in which I place my trust.

I rightfully inherited the throne of this kingdom and empire from my parents, who had been dispossessed, but I had to take it as well, and in the taking and in the years before, I was a child of the poor, I lived in the mountains, I knew war. These are the things that have made me, and I cannot ever leave them behind.

We fought in the highlands, the forests, and on the plain. The city itself was a battleground (first when we besieged it, and then when we defended it), and during the initial years of the revolt the wind often brought the smell of smoke from burning houses, streets, or whole districts. Archers would strike at their pleasure, extinguishing lives as if they were at target practice. And for years the wooded areas within the city walls were crowded with refugees in shantytowns where fires burned all night but were never quite strong enough in winter to keep the children warm. From the palace, their deficiencies unknown, the fires looked merely beautiful.

Though I myself have seen so many battles I can hardly tell one from another, far worse than any battle was to take leave of your father when he left to fight. All the suffering of these years seemed to lie in the moment when our outstretched hands would part and either he or I would turn to ride away. Even now he is riding with the Damavand, the horsemen from whom I am descended, whose land is on the outer reach of the kingdom as it vanishes into the Veil of Snows. Detachments of soldiers and caravans of merchants who fall into the Veil of Snows may be lost forever, or may return in confusion years later, knowing neither where they have been nor for how long. Those who come back seldom are remembered, for by the time they return, no one of their generation remains.

Though Damavand generals sometimes drive their enemy deep into the turbulence of the snows, they cannot pursue. Should they spur their horses into the looming gorges or out onto the infinite snowfields, they simply disappear.

Your father is now with the armies in the high peaks of the Damavand. I learned from having fought in the last great battle, at the edge of all we know, that when you ride in the shadows of those mountains something in your heart draws you to them as if they were black water flowing hypnotically beneath a bridge. Once you have ventured into that country, only if you have a great deal of life in you can you resist going too close, for as you lift your head to stare at clouds of ice swirling above blinding snowfields, you feel as pleasurable a tide as if you were standing in the surf in June.

When you ride with Damavand cavalry, time has no meaning, life flows with the speed and power of a mountain torrent, necessity dictates all, and the heart is keyed to the blood of horses that canter for days in wind and snow. In the last battle, your father and I commanded the two armies that harried the battalions of the usurper, a man, my ancient enemy, whose name I will neither utter nor write. That I will never say his name I promised to the tutor, who taught me not to dwell on evil. Who is the tutor? You owe your life to him, as I owe mine.

In the last battle we pushed the usurper's soldiers so hard against the Veil of Snows that their formations melted into the ice, their ranks were eaten by mist, their cries swallowed by silence. We fought so close and so fiercely that we lost track of time, and we watched as half our soldiers passed from this world into the world of the wind.

And at the very end my heart grew still as I stood on a distant crest while your father and the usurper fought upon a high cornice half hidden by curtains of glassy snow. Blinded by sun flashing against snow and ice, I thought your father would be taken to the other side, but as he fell and the usurper was about to strike, a tongue of ragged cloud swept across them, luffing the usurper's black robes, and when the field was white again and shone with sun, only your father remained.

This was our blessing, but it was just the last of many gifts of providence, and, like all good things, impermanent. As stars rise, they fall, and as they fall, they rise, which is why your father has encamped with thousands of horsemen in the valleys near the tree line and the high lakes. He watches even when it seems that nothing will come, for we ourselves have seen that fortune does not stick in place, and the prospect of your birth has driven him to great care.

91

Now the snow that when I was young rushed past my face like maddened swarms of insects lies quietly upon my palace roofs, dampening footfalls below in halls of marble and softening the noise from courtyards as large as city squares. Streams of smoke from my chimneys rise peacefully and straight.

It was not always as it is. Not long ago this dream of peace moved me so as the object of my prayers that I grieved for it as if for a lost love, but now that I have it in hand the days of war flood upon my memory in honor and grace.

Why have I spent my life at war? Why does this time of peace seem unnatural? And how did all this come to pass? Through love, and loyalty, and memory that reaches into places I have never been.

Until my ninth year I lived in perfect innocence in a perfect place. The air was clear, the sun shone bright, and the hay was dry and blond. It all might have remained that way, but as soon as my heart began to stir and I began to wonder about the city on the plain, the tutor broke the undisturbed perfection and told me my history, as if to see me born before his eyes.

My father, he said, was the heir to the throne, and my mother a princess of the Damavand whose parents had been murdered by the usurper when she was an infant. Slain by archers in the courtyard of an inn, my grandparents had covered my mother with their bodies as they died, and because she was inexplicably silent, the assassins thought they had killed her.

But she was unhurt, and a maid at the inn retrieved the baby and carried her deep into the forest. She was never to return to the country of the Damavand. Nor was she ever to set foot in the city from which she had been spirited. Instead, accident and fate brought my father to her in the forest — my father, who was a prince, and she, who was a princess. But their time together would be short, for soon after I was born they, too, were murdered: the cause of the first war that split the kingdom. Pushed by a detachment of archers to the edge of a precipice above a lake, they chose to die in a fall rather than be pierced by half a hundred crossbow bolts.

I am, then, the second child who has not known her parents, the second child whose mother and father were taken from her by this same man whom we have now conquered but not killed, whom we have driven into the Veil of Snows, and for whom we watch day by day.

The maid who had saved my mother had to flee yet again. Knowing that I was her queen, she carried me into the South Mountains, where the Veil of Snows does not touch, where it is more beautiful and tranquil than language can describe, and where I spent my childhood with no hint of who I was or how I had come into the world. I was loved and I was happy, but though I was not yet ten years of age I knew that the heart needs a trigger of imperfection to be made whole. I hungered for the sight of a great thing, or the taking of a great chance, or the making of a great sacrifice.

The tutor, whom I called grandfather until the day I discovered that he was not of my own blood, knew that I would go. He knew that, once I had found out my past, love and loyalty would rise as if from nothing, and that I would enter a great city (I had never seen even a town) where as a ten-year-old child I would set about overthrowing a regime that enjoyed perfect and detailed control of absolutely everything.

When the tutor told the tale, I did not understand my part in it until the very end, but then all came clear. I could not have loved my mother and father more in the flesh than as they were presented in his story. Perhaps I loved them more because they were lost. As you will discover, the greatest love is for those who are lost.

How could I have left him, this man who raised me? How could I have gone to overthrow a king? How could I, so young? I don't know, but I began my journey to the city in blindness and confidence, which, if you think of it, is how we must all live, given the nature of our origin and the certainty of our destination.

I left in the fall, after harvest. I cried to leave the tutor, for, as he had vowed never to return to the city on the plain, I thought I might never see him again. I was afraid of the darkness and the road. I dreaded the wild boar, the wolf, and bear. And I had no idea what I would find in the city or what to do when I found it. But I left just the same. I had no choice. That I was so young did not matter. The usurper had forced the spirit of my family behind a high and heavenly dam, and when the dam broke, the spirit of my family came flooding down.

We were three days' walk from the nearest track. Guided by the North Star, I crossed the flanks of the mountains through tall forests dimly lit and over meadows above the timberline, where the snow can be a foot deep while on the plain the lakes are as warm as a bath.

In seemingly never-ending glades of birch and laurel I twice stumbled onto wild boar so much larger than I that I felt as if I were in the presence of a kind of whale. I had no strategy, no power, no recourse, and no retreat, so I did what I could. I scolded them for startling me, shaking a finger at them and slightly tilting my head as I spoke. And these creatures, who singly have destroyed squadrons of mounted

hunters, bowed their heads and crouched as if they were shamed by my reprimand. Perhaps it was because, being less than an arm's length from the grotesque mouths out of which bristled their curling tusks, I was the first being other than those of their own kind who had actually looked deep into their eyes. Though it was many years ago, I remember that the eyes are as weak and watery as the body of the boar is strong and hard.

On my second day on the road I met a caravan of merchants heading for the South Mountains, where they had never been. A dozen of them were traveling with a hundred snow-white mules — I had never seen a horse or a mule. They were so terrified of the great forests and high passes that had been my refuge, and so shamed by my cheerful assurances, that they offered me a mule on which to finish my journey.

"It will take ten days," they said, "to reach the city's south gates. The mule is slow and deliberate, but still faster than you."

So it was that I pacified wild boar, first saw a road, and entered the city. In my ten days' ride I had feared that the things that were happening to me had robbed me of my will and my power, for the road led, the mule carried, in the forest the weather had been compassionate, and the boar had slunk back as if behind me were an angel with a sword.

Never before had I been in a city. I was surprised to find that the walls and towers I had seen as I approached were not the only row of buildings, and that the city was deeper than it was wide. At first, things were not easy. For example, I had always greeted everyone I met. The tutor and Anna the maid were the only people I had ever known. In fact, except for a hunter who once stumbled

onto our cabin when I was small, and the merchants I had just met on the road, they were the only people I had ever *seen*. So I politely greeted every person that I passed. As I encountered thousands upon thousands of people going about their business in the streets, I said, "Hello. How are you?" to each of them. It was exhausting, and because I was too young to have been a politician, they assumed that I was insane.

I said hello to everyone until I was too worn to speak, and no one, not one person, responded. Were it not for ruffians who pushed me and snatched at my dress, I would have begun to suspect that I did not exist.

So rapidly and completely assaulted were each of my senses that I hadn't the time to miss home. To right and to left, up and down, above and below, things were continually happening. I found this overwhelming, because in the forest things happened only every two weeks or so. Not here. Here, men swallowed fire and swords. I had never seen anyone swallow a sword: I had never seen a sword. Recreant women were placed in stocks and dipped in pools of icy water, their husbands tied to stakes while for a tenth of a gold Rothbart anyone who pleased could throw pies or fruit cocktails at them.

A thousand vendors lined each broad boulevard, and the whole city was a vast kitchen in which donkey meat, and wurst, and worse, were turned on rotisseries powered by sullen rats running on treadmills in pursuit of ever elusive chunks of Turkish taffy. The muskrat kebobs and crow nuggets were only part of it. On every corner, cauldrons competed to offer soups as fetid as infantrymen's socks, and treacherous pet handlers offered their birds or gerbils for frying, baking, or whatever you please. The selection was limitless. Eventually, I would hardly even take notice when at one stand or another whole woodchucks were consumed on the half-shell, as the vendor screamed, "The trick is in the sauce! The trick is in the sauce!"

Mad souls sold everything. They sold small ugly trinkets that did nothing, cloaks of painstakingly stretched bee hides, land in countries that did not exist, combination megaphones and dental picks, small creatures trapped in bottles, oics (whatever they were), pictures, elixirs, snapdragons, flagons, sponges, chariots, bells, mattresses, plungers, and lariats, folding furniture, singing lessons, chalk, rope, pigs, wigs, and weapons of war. The Tookistrasse was devoted exclusively to stores that specialized in only four items each. One, for example, sold Swedish medical books, lemons, arrowheads, and bassoons. Another sold balls of ambergris, pictures of ancient philosophers, chocolate pretzels, and wire mesh.

To scare up business, each storekeeper stood in front of his establishment and screamed about his wares until his eyes popped and his face was the color of a cherry. You knew that they had become so accustomed to this that they did it not because they wanted to sell their ambergris or gray flannel exercise pants but because they could do nothing else. In fact, on one of the streets that together led like a hundred thousand rivers into the palace square, I passed a great building that in other countries might have been a central post office or the ministry of the interior. Here, it was an old-age home for the merchants of the Tookistrasse and some of the other great commercial avenues, and its countless windows, rising hundreds of feet and extending along the length of a building that took five minutes to traverse at the pace of a mule trotting like a bug to its stable, were filled with ancient merchants still as red as cherries, eyes popped almost all the way to Bolivia, screaming automatically of latex carriage mats, nut bars, mechanical pillows, and nose-correction clamps.

And all this was but the prelude to the chaos, the color, and the music of the palace square at dusk. I didn't then know the meaning of hopelessness, or of desire, elation, or defeat. But when I felt them swirling together entwined in the open space above the square I understood immediately what they meant, as they fused into one strong cry of the heart. In the palace square the open space was like an ocean of freedom for a people otherwise oppressed, and the airy sea to which they came each evening to await events lapped against seemingly infinite walls of stone.

Here were defiance and freedom, but all in chains. And the two mixed like the warm currents of wind that spiraled up from the great bonfires and tumbled through the winter air.

Roman candles were launched from a hundred different points, exploding like the destruction of heaven, and drops of fire poured down from walls, towers, and the tops of trees. Who poured the flaming oils that hissed threats and dissatisfaction before they disappeared, and why? I never found out, and it has not happened since the rebellion.

Full orchestras played the remembered music of empire, music that was written no longer, and in one corner of the square a plain of ice that from high in the palace must have seemed no bigger than a speck held ten thousand delirious skaters gliding in unison to the music of an orchestra of at least half their number. Flames glowed from tripods set upon the ice in long lines that, like railway rails, came together only in illusion. And here and there, in pockets of silence, a single couple might be seen, skating together through the shadows.

A million people were in the palace square, their upturned faces lost in a fume of luminous white that churned against the gray smoke of dusk. And here I left the snow-white mule, dismounting as he continued on, for I thought that I had found the center of the world.

As soon as I alighted I realized that music and the wind were not the only sounds I had been hearing. The streets were awash in whispering that sounded like the flow of water in small streams, or wind that lashes the pines and courses through their needles like sea foam. The whole nation had been put in exile by one man, and yet no one had gone anywhere. People spoke in short, clipped, guarded exchanges, or they whispered.

Given the nature of that which was cooked, it was hard to be hungry, but after a few hours wandering in the knee-high surf of whispering, and after following the motion of the skaters as they sailed in and out of flames and shadows with the damaged grace and dark electricity of the aurora, I was chilled and feverish and I desperately wanted something to eat. I had been in the freezing air for many days, and though the wind had made me strong and my eyes burned with the new, I wanted to come in from the cold.

Not only did I have no money, I had never seen money. Though the tutor had hurriedly explained it as I left, his thoughts were sometimes unduly compressed. Even if they were not like the mad whispering beneath the walls, they often eluded me. Money, as I understood it from his breathless dissertation, was defined primarily by its velocity. It was, like anything else, a commodity that rose or fell in value even if it were in itself a measure of value. The essence, he had said, was convertibility. This led him into a complicated essay on price theory. All very well and good, but I hadn't the slightest idea of what he was talking about.

When I came to a vast bakery in the open square I simply asked if I could have some bread. "As much as you'd like," said a man so strange that I couldn't take my eyes from him. He was tall and thin, with a bulbous, hooked nose, and shaggy camel-colored hair. His huge eyes were composed of concentric circles the color of tiger stripes, and every time he spoke he smiled. Though in the future he would protect me, I felt upon looking at his sloping shoulders and his gangly neck that, somehow, I had to protect him.

"I'll take ten, please."

"A quarter Rothbart and a tenth weasel gold ducat."

"What?" I asked.

He repeated the price as I stood in place, uncomprehending.

"Are you from elsewhere?"

I nodded.

"From the West Plain?"

"No."

"From the Prairie of Salt?"

"No."

"Uh, from the Gulf of Tizla?"

"No."

"From the forests?"

"Yes."

"A forest girl!" He was stunned. Virtually no one lived in the forests anymore, and those who did were valued as islands of tranquility, touchstones of the past, being completely ignorant of the troubles that had made life in the kingdom so ugly and bleak. Of course, I was not at all ignorant of these, but he could not have known that. "Wait," he said. "I'll get Notorincus. Meanwhile, eat." He pushed a tray of hot bread in my direction, and it held me in front of his stand like a magnet.

A loaf and a half later, he returned with Notorincus. I wasn't sure that, like the tall one, Astrahn, Notorincus was human. Whereas Astrahn was slim and buff colored, Notorincus was a squat, stocky ball, with rich black hair cut like fur. It did not lie or fall like human hair, but stood in palisades, as in a pelt or a cut rug. His eyes were slightly crossed, his face round. Most remarkable was his mouth, for this man who at first was too abashed to look anyone in the eyes had two glacially white beaver teeth in the center of his shy smile.

He was Notorincus, a bakery slave, and Astrahn was a slave's slave, which was rather low on the social scale but much in demand, as every slave wanted above all a slave of his own, and the masters, who were themselves slaves of the nobility, who were themselves slaves of the usurper, were happy to double their work force. Astrahn and Notorincus were two of a vast number of bakery slaves, of which at least a third were slave's slaves. The slave's slaves had been told that the usurper would soon establish a new position — the slave of the slave of a slave — and this kept them happy in their days as slaves of slaves.

But Astrahn and Notorincus were slaves only in name, for they had taken the oath of rebellion, something of which I had not even heard, something of which even the tutor had not heard, as it had been established long after his exile. Like the mad whispering, the oath moved no stones, burned no treasuries, and loosed no arrows, but it put the oath takers in a state of expectation and it freed their souls.

"Duck under the counter," Notorincus said. Never having heard this expression, I looked under the counter, expecting to see a duck. Then he said, "Come quickly." Though I wasn't sure that I should, I did. They took me closer to the ovens, and by the light of a myrrh fire they gave me soup and bread. They wanted news of the outside, beyond the struggle, news that I could not provide, because, as far as I knew, nothing had ever happened to me.

Had they asked me about myself, and had I been willing to answer, the rebellion might have started that day, and far too early. But they were caught in the wave of things, and they asked questions that did

not lead home. Quite apart from that, the tutor had forbidden me to reveal who I was before the time was right.

"And when will the time be right?" I had asked.

His reply was, "When the whole people is like a great stone at the top of a hill, and it seems as if even the wind might rock the stone over the edge to begin its force-filled descent."

With no idea that Astrahn and Notorincus had taken the oath of rebellion, or even of the oath itself, I ate my soup and answered their questions not as if I were an owl but as if I were an otter.

"What forest did you come from?" asked Astrahn.

"The only forest I know, and I know only the forest."

"The forest of the South Mountains?"

"Where I started was for me the center. I have advanced from the center, but in which direction I do not know."

"Where did the sun come up as you made your way, on the right or on the left?" Notorincus asked, helpfully, and, of course, slyly. He turned deep red.

"It was cloudy."

"In what direction, then," Astrahn prodded, "was the North Star?"

"North," I said.

"Was it behind you? To your left? Your right? Ahead?"

This inquisition was child's play compared to the tutor's Pythagorean examinations. The tutor had been the chief of the royal academies and libraries, and in my first nine years I had been his only student, the sole recipient of his discourses, and the lone disciple of his drills. Though I didn't know how lucky I was to be the single interlocutor of such a brilliant man, I did know a great deal else, from physics and mathematics to the history of art and the theory of music. Only in certain practical matters and in social discourse,

for which we had no need in our splendid isolation, was I deficient. In answer to Astrahn's question I stated that "On some days, the North Star was on my right."

"Aha!" he said.

"And on some days, it was to my left."

"Oh."

"And sometimes it was behind me, though at other times it was in front."

"Oh, oh, oh," said Notorincus, his eyes more crossed than usual.

"Most of the time, though," I offered naively, as if to clinch the matter, "it was directly overhead."

"Well," Notorincus said, spreading his arms and turning up his hands, "tell us about the forests."

"Ah," I said, "they were beautiful."

"Is that all?"

"And they were green."

"Ask her about animals, Notorincus. You know about animals. You'll be able to tell that way."

"Good idea," said Notorincus, and then he cleared his throat. "Ahagghham! What animals lived in this green forest?"

"My!" I said. "So many animals."

"Tell us about them."

"My favorite," I declared, "was the spoffet-toed chowgis."

"I don't know that one," Notorincus said.

"We fished for mavrodaphnic seacats."

"In sweet water?"

"In brine wundels and sodium freshets."

"What about birds?"

"What about them?"

109

"Eagles, crows, owls, pigeons?"

"Let's see. Uh, no. Whistlenots, windowbangers, and monument foulers."

"Put it this way," Notorincus said to Astrahn. "If she's an agent of the usurper, his tactics have changed."

"All right," said Astrahn, "I agree. We'll get right to the point."

I sat coyly, saying nothing.

Astrahn turned to me. "Ahem!"

"Yes?"

"Were there armies of rebels in your neighborhood?"

"In the forest?"

"Yes."

"No."

"Were there ... small bands?"

"No."

"Individuals?"

"No."

"Not a single rebel?"

"What are rebels?"

"Men that soldiers chase. Men who are hungry and tired and wounded. Men with scars and broken hearts and families destroyed or left behind."

"Once," I said, "a hunter came. He asked directions, and I gave him a bag of mushrooms."

"He asked *you* directions?"

"Yes."

"Good luck to him."

"He was the only person I had ever met until last week on the road."

"Which road?"

"The road that led here."

"From where?"

"From where I came."

"You met someone on the road?"

"Yes, merchants."

"Where were they going?"

"They were going to the place from which I had come."

"And where is that?"

"I don't know."

"This little girl can't help the rebellion," announced Astrahn. "Mentally, she's a spoffet-toed chowgis."

"I suppose you're right, Astrahn, but she's uncorrupted, she goes without the usurper's mark, and it is our duty to protect her."

"Protect me from *what?*" I asked.

In the instant before their answer we were shaken by a tremendous explosion. All changed. Everyone froze momentarily, overcome by fear. Then the music stopped and the skaters dropped to the ice and frantically began to unlace their skates. Lights started to go out, and from every direction came the sounds of running.

Suddenly a huge red fire began to burn in the sky above, coloring the frozen city with the hue of blood. An immense flare lofted by a trench mortar now descended slowly under a parachute, swinging to and fro like a jailer's keys.

In red light so bright that it hurt my eyes, I saw everyone running. "What is it?" I asked.

"Don't you know?" Notorincus said as he and Astrahn struggled to gather up their baking tools. "How long have you been here?"

"I arrived at dusk today."

"It's curfew," Astrahn said. "The square must be clear in five minutes; in ten minutes, the first ring of the city; in fifteen, the second ring; and so on. Within half an hour all the rings of the city will be absolutely empty, so the usurper can ride through the streets at night in his chariot, clad in his black robes, and kill anyone he sees. And anywhere that he is not, his soldiers are, doing their best to imitate their master."

Even though Astrahn and Notorincus hurried and were about to break away, I asked, "What is the purpose of emptying the streets? Is it just so the usurper can ride through a dead city?"

"Control," said Astrahn. "Every night he must prove to himself that his power is absolute, and every night he does."

Though the usurper had killed my parents and grandparents, though I was only ten years of age, though he rode in a chariot and I was unarmed, and though he had killed long before I was born, even before my mother or father were born, I was not afraid. I cannot tell you why, but I simply was not afraid. They say now that it was in my blood, but I say that it was a gift from a kingdom far and clear.

"Where are you staying?" shouted Notorincus. "You must arrive there within three minutes!"

"I'm not staying anywhere," I said, calmly.

"Oh no!" they both shouted. "We can't take you in, because we already have seventeen. One more and the compartment will be so full they'll smother. You must find a hiding place."

"I'm not afraid of the usurper," I said.

They stopped dead, even as precious time was passing, even at risk to their lives, for they had never heard these words before.

From the far end of the palace square came the thunder of a phalanx of cavalry a mile wide. Though distant, they approached at a gallop.

"You may not be afraid," Notorincus cried as we began to run once again, "but if the usurper sees you he'll kill you. And if the soldiers catch you they'll bring you to selection. We bake in the palace, and we know secrets. Listen carefully. At selection, tell them that you're a yam curler."

"A what?" I asked, but they were swept away from me on tides of panic, and as I ran I remembered the words *yam curler* though I did not know what they meant. Nor did I know what Notorincus meant by selection.

The awful red light descended, and even as I sought the shadows I could feel its heat against my back. The cavalry came like a tidal wave, tramping down the snow until the square behind them glinted, until the surface was so smooth that wind-propelled remnants of timber and tent cloth were swept along like reeds blown across the ice.

In the forest we had had none of the entertainments common to cities, and if those we had were somewhat idiosyncratic, they were excellent preparation for life as it has unfolded. One of my games, for example, was to lie on the ice of a mountain lake until I could no longer feel the cold. Thus, as the evening passed, I was not uncomfortable in the frigid air.

Though I was unfamiliar with the social graces, and dancing, and what was in a zoo, a bakery, or a museum, on a clear day when I had neither lessons nor work I would run in the mountains sometimes from dawn until dark. In short order I would reach the state of perfect balance in which running up a mountain slope seemed to require no effort, running on the flat was like riding, and to run downhill was to fly.

Thus, as others had fled the palace square in gales of emphysema,

I left as fast and easily as a mounted rider. Long before the start of curfew I had bounded to the Fifth Ring of the city, where all was quiet and everyone had gone to bed. The prosperous noblemen of the Fifth Ring did not, like everyone else, go to the palace square at night. Instead, they had early dinner parties and sat by their fires, on silken chairs, drinking whiskey and reading biographies of the usurper.

I knocked half-heartedly on a few doors, knowing that no one within would open them on a winter night after curfew. I imagined that at times other people too had been driven into the Fifth Ring, with soldiers trailing not far behind. And those who live in warmth on the far side of oaken doors usually have lost their taste for combat so long before and so completely that they do not even like to witness it, much less throw themselves to its mercies.

For a few moments I drifted about, admiring the lovely houses, the flawless iron fences, the iced-over brooks in serpentine parks with gilded bridges, and then I heard the distant sound of horses.

Not far up the street were some garbage bins, which I thought were for housing animals or storing grain. I went to the first one, opened it, and turned away, trying to keep my stomach down. In a city where it was fashionable to eat virtually anything, the garbage can had been stuffed with giraffe innards. The second was even worse, but then I saw another one overflowing with excelsior.

The cedar excelsior was as clean and fragrant as the other bins' contents had been nauseating. I lifted the top and burrowed in. It was warm and comfortable, and I yawned. It seemed a fit place to try to sleep, and I almost did fall asleep, but then a group of horses and riders rounded the corner. Feeling entirely invisible, I thought the best way to hide was simply to go limp. If I slept I would be calm, and they would go away.

I was awakened much later, when I was much colder, by voices and the sound of horseshoes against the cobbles.

"That's excelsior," said one of the voices. "They use it to wrap delicate objects. Because it's in front of the house of a nobleman, there might be something valuable in it, that the unpackers overlooked. Wolfgang, Bonticlaw, turn it over and pull out the packing."

I heard two men leap from their horses, and boots on the stone. I closed my eyes as I was turned upside down and rolled out into the night air on a breaking wave of excelsior.

Hands tied behind my back, I rode folded over the hindquarters of a horse. As we had ridden along the main radial of the Fifth Ring, we had joined a cavalry detachment of fifty. Some of the cavalrymen had captives, and some wore blood-spattered clothes. They were happy and proud, but I could hardly bear to look at them. I wondered if I had been right to come to this place, to leave behind the gentle life I had had in the mountains, when sometimes I would see the moon from my bed, voluminous and yellow, floating over distant snowfields.

Just before midnight — I could tell by the position of the very same moon, which now seemed cold and cruel — we had come through an industrial district in the Third Ring, where all you could hear was the roar of fires and the sound of metal striking metal. As we were about to cross a bridge over a canal, the commander of the detachment called a halt. So quickly did the horses stop that I was thrown against the chain mail of my captor and I watched some cavalrymen fall from their saddles.

"Back in!" came the cry all the way down the line. "Honor his coming!"

The horses sidled and kicked. The men pushed them and swore. But in less than a minute the troop had formed itself into rows on either side of the road. The horses were forced to their knees, the men went there as volunteers, and when the lines were completely straight the soldiers hung their heads as if in shame. Then I heard what the commander had heard earlier at the head of his troop — the sound of steel wheels rushing over roads and cobbles. The air was so disturbed that it moaned and shrieked as if with the clash of a hundred swords.

"All bow!" the commander screamed, and every soldier and most of the horses bent their heads. In the bright moonlight it seemed that fifty gleaming silver spheres had been put upon fifty supernatural bodies, and the light glinted off helmets and weapons like the spray of a waterfall dashing upon ice-encrusted rock.

As the usurper's chariot rattled over the bridge, the noise became deafening. No one was supposed to look at him, least of all someone like me, and the penalty for transgression was death. But, once, I had been miraculously spared, as had my mother, and I acted accordingly.

While the soldiers might see only a hoof or the lower part of a wheel, I saw him, I looked directly at his face, and I did not fear. He was tall and heavy, and his boots made him seem even taller as he stood on the platform of a chariot that thundered past as if we did not exist. His face was scarred and twisted, his towering form draped in black robes that flew in his wake like the wings of a crow that dies in midair and cartwheels to the ground. He wore a mask that made him look like death itself. The wind that followed him was cold, and his own soldiers feared him so much that they held their heads down until their chins pressed against their breastplates.

When I saw that he was real, I determined to dispatch him into the

black world whence he had come. I have yet to kill him, and I collect armies now the way other people bring wood to the stove. Someday, he will come back, and I will have my chance. We rode on.

As one detachment joined another we became part of a great river of horses and men. I have seen such things a thousand times since, and still they impress me. Then, it was new, I was a child and a captive, and I was amazed by the might and the force.

At a barracks near the palace square my hands were unlashed, I was removed from the horse, and they put me in a wooden wagon that held whole families — fathers, mothers, children, grandparents, and even dogs. As soon as the door was closed the light disappeared and the only way to know that the others were still present was to hear the mothers comforting their softly crying babies.

"Where are they taking us?" I asked the darkness, and no one answered. I asked again, and no one would break the silence. I was a child, and it was for the children's sake that I received no answer.

At dusk the next day the door slid open and we left the wagon in disarray. Half of us were sick and feverish already, though not I. Others, having had neither water nor food, moved almost as weakly as the sick. Our worst enemy, however, was neither sickness nor lack of food and water, but the cold.

We were in a snowy forest that dusk had colored gray. The pines were still and the spaces between them mysterious. To our left was a group of low buildings and to our right a factory with six chimneys from which issued six streams of dark smoke that came together in an angry coil and then split off on currents of wind to disappear forever among the clouds.

"Line up," we were told, and we did. We filed slowly into a building,

and when at last I stepped inside, one of the soldiers simply picked me up and threw me across the room, where other children had also been thrown, and lay crying.

I was the first to be selected. An enormous soldier picked me up, immobilized my arms, and carried me to the man at the table.

I didn't like the look of him, and I didn't like the look on the soldiers' faces, but, still, I was unafraid.

"And what were you doing out in the Fifth Ring after curfew, dear?" asked the man at the table. Had it not been for Astrahn and Notorincus, I dare not imagine what might have happened to me, but I knew exactly what to say.

"Curling yams," I said. "I was on my way to a yam curling job. I'm a yam curler."

He was dumbstruck. Evidently, in removing one pleasure I had substituted another, and he didn't know quite what to do. He motioned with his pen, and I was hustled out a door to a little yard, and back into a wagon. I lay on the floor, and through a crack in the boards I could see people in the line, but only the part of them between knee and thigh. I saw shawls, and suitcases, and children of all sizes moving as slowly as a river until they were eaten by the dusk and I could no longer tell the difference between the color gray, the black of night, the feeling of cold, the smell of smoke, and my own dark sleep.

The next I knew, it was daylight. Shivering and filthy, I was removed from the wagon by a red-haired middle-aged woman in a white tunic and chef's hat. I had the feeling that, though I had no idea of what a yam might be, she did.

Snow fell all around us and salted the air between my face and

120

hers. The sleeves of my coat were glazed with snowflakes that shone in the gray light of the sky. I was deep inside the palace itself, in the courtyard of the yam kitchens, where wagons came by the thousand to unload yams of many colors. This courtyard was so big that you would need a full minute to gallop a good horse along any one of its sides. The wagons came and went through four tunnels, and walls of lighted windows rose into the dim reaches of falling snow.

"This is the yam section of the starch kitchens," she said. "We are responsible for yam output. Other regions handle potatoes, rices, and crusts for meat pies. The crusts were a great gift that the old emperor took from the bakers and gave to the starch section, in the time when we had empty rooms and idle hands."

"All those sacks of yam flour are for the crusts of meat pies?" I asked, eyeing a loggia upon which lay a pile of ten-thousand flour sacks marked, "Flour, Yam, Type II: Destination — Crust Division, Meat Pie Sector."

"Those are for the luncheon in recognition of the slavish obedience of the Duke of Tookisheim. The Duke of Tookisheim's newspapers are the most adoring of the emperor. In one issue of the *Tookisheim Post* alone, the emperor and his wife were depicted as divine beings fourteen hundred times. It taxed the engravers even more than does the government."

"Isn't that disgusting?" I asked. "Isn't it vile that the Duke of Took-isheim is so contemptuous of the truth?"

"Ssshh!" she said, putting her finger to her lips. "Don't say the in-correct word."

"What incorrect word?"

"The word you said."

"Truth?"

"Ssshh! That word was abolished years ago. It got in the way. It hurt the Duke of Tookisheim's feelings, because when there was that other newspaper, they used the incorrect word to make war on the emperor and to make fun of the Duke of Tookisheim and his brilliant young son, Peanut. But the Duke of Tookisheim knew what to do. He drove that other newspaper into bolivian."

"Why didn't the emperor just close it down?"

"He let the Duke of Tookisheim and Peanut defeat it fairly and squarely, so no one could say he was a bad emperor. In the end, each issue of the *Tookisheim Post* weighed more than a horse. It had a section to suit everyone. We loved the yam articles in the starch section. And the Duke of Tookisheim's journalists were the best in the world at repeating things. The other newspaper might say *Ox*, but the Duke of Tookisheim's newspaper would say *No Ox! No Ox! No Ox! No Ox! No Ox! No Ox! No Ox! No Ox!*, again and again and again, until, even if an ox had been standing on your head you would be convinced that there was no ox, no ox, no ox, no ox, no ... oh, excuse me."

"Ox," I said, thinking that this woman might have been more than what met the eye.

"Now, we *all* love the emperor. The emperor can do no wrong. The emperor is good. He is a genius. He loves us all. He will live forever. The old emperor was bad. The old emperor was selfish. You know, the emperor freed us from the old emperor."

"Yes, I know," I said. She was speaking of my grandfather.

"He slew him."

"I thought the old emperor died a natural death."

"Did he?" She laughed. "I don't know! I don't know!" she said cheerfully. "All I know is what the Duke of Tookisheim tells me!" She winked. It might have been frightening. There were many like her,

but she was not what she appeared to be. Eventually I learned that she was a friend of Astrahn and Notorincus, and that she, too, had taken the oath of rebellion. But we were in the palace itself, where love of the new emperor was mandatory. And yet the only real love of the emperor came from the emperor himself, and other than that, all opinions were creatures of falsity and fear, even if not everyone knew, even if the Duke of Tookisheim's and Peanut's thorough repetitions had done their work of hypnosis.

"The bakeries are on our east wall," said Elena, the pretending admirer of the Duke of Tookisheim. "They are much bigger than the yam kitchens, of course. Well, naturally. And the chocolate kitchens are on the south wall. Though the chocolate kitchens have six thousand chefs and workers and we have only three thousand, they are divided by law into three sections — beverages, candy, and desserts. So, really, we are bigger than they, especially as the dessert section of the chocolate kitchen is half under the jurisdiction of the bakers."

Here is where I chose to penetrate her veil. "Bakers?" I asked. "Would you happen to have made the acquaintance of one Astrahn and one Notorincus?"

She burst into an idiotic peal of soprano laughter and rushed to embrace me. But as I recoiled, she whispered, four octaves lower, "Shut up, my dear. People are listening. All in good time."

"You must tell me," I responded, dropping as many octaves as I could (because of my age I was still far to the right of the *Steinweg*), "what, in God's name, is a yam curler. What is a yam? I don't want to go back to selection."

"A yam, you see," she told me, "is the edible starchy tuberous root of the various plants of the genus *Dioscorea* (as in *D. Sativa*, or *D. Alata*) that largely replaces the potato as a staple food in tropical climates and is cooked in the same way but has coarser flesh."

123

"Oh."

"It is necessary for everyone in the yam kitchen to know that, lest he be accidentally sequestered to the yak kitchen."

"What is a yak?"

"A big animal, like a buffalo, but it looks less like a French poodle and more like a grass hut."

"What is a yam *curler?*"

"In time, my dear, you will wish that you had never heard the word."

Then she took me on a tour of the yam kitchens. Never having heard of a yam, I had had no way of knowing that it existed in several hundred varieties. A score of these were being prepared for the Duke of Tookisheim's lunch the next day, it being well known that Peanut was a big yam lover. Master carvers made of yams detailed representations of castles, angels, galleons, barges, and trees. I thought this was yam curling, and I swallowed hard, because I couldn't whittle.

Again the peals of soprano laughter. Again the conspiratorial drop in octaves, as we went from one huge yam hall to another. "A yam curler, my dear," she said as she glanced left and right to check for prying eyes, "does not carve. Curling a yam means standing on the yam sorting apron as the yams roll down, and sweeping the paths in front of them with a broom."

"That's all?"

"Don't underestimate it," she said. "You must know several hundred types of yams, their trajectories and destinations, their coefficients of friction and how they roll over the dust of all the other yams. The permutations are staggering. I hope you can calculate in your head."

I looked at her as if we both were crazy.

"The danger, too. The yam sorting apron has a variable slope. On humid days or before a royal lunch, it is slightly steepened. You can slip and roll into any one of dozens of choppers, peelers, cauldrons, ovens, or, God help you, into the yam disposal shaft, which falls two hundred feet into a pit simply seething with tremendous, horrendous, yam-eating — aahhs!" she said, unable to repeat the name of whatever it was that consumed the broken and imperfect yams.

"We'll get you set up," she told me. "Before ascending to your room, you can take a long hot bath in slightly yammish parboiling water, change into clean clothes, and have something to eat. Tonight the yam workers are having woodchuck pie with yam salad and yam pudding."

"Ascending to my room?"

"The dormitories are full, so I'm afraid you'll have to sleep in a little room in the tower. It's very cold there, but we managed to salvage — steal, actually — a new featherbed that was mistakenly delivered to the starch courtyard. It had been on its way to one of Peanut Tookisheim's sycophants, and is three feet thick. The stairs to the tower collapsed when the old emperor's astronomical telescope was smashed, so you'll have to ride up on a rope."

"Why was his telescope smashed?"

"The new emperor does not want us to look beyond what happens in his kingdom. He says it is wrong and useless. He hates the stars because he cannot ever hope to govern them, so they are now incorrect. Don't say the word in public. Don't admit to having looked into the night sky."

I bathed in a huge vat of only slightly yammish hot water, was given a yam curler's black velvet dress trimmed with orange silks, had a fulsome meal of woodchuck pie, and went to the tower, where Elena comforted me before my counterweighted ascent. The shaft above disappeared into its own length and darkness, but I was not afraid, as

I had grown up in the mountains and frequently gone with the goats to places most little girls could not even dream of. It took ten minutes of steady rising to get to my chamber at the top, the very chamber in which I am now writing down my story for you.

I spun gently on the rope and passed window after window through which I could see swirling snow and a golden sun clothed in frozen light.

This little room as I first saw it was not what it is now, after royal artisans have filled the cracks, reglazed the windows, laid a new floor, and enameled the walls and moldings until, years after the paint was applied, it still looks wet. In those days it was perpetually cold as the wind shrieked through the cracks. The floor was rotten, the walls peeling, and every surface covered by spider webs and grime.

But I could still see through the windows high above the city, the lake, and the palace. I threw one open, and looked out on the palace side. As the bitter air flowed in and magnetized to the floor, what I saw was so astonishing that it became impossible to think of comfort. Horsemen and couriers who rode from place to place upon the palace roofs would head for the distance in any direction and soon pass from sight. So many chimneys spouted smoke that I felt like an Arctic captain surveying a patch of rigid emerald sea where all the whales of the world had gathered in a mighty fleet. Now and then, a figure would emerge from a door and step onto the roof to shake out a mop, release a pigeon, or take a breath of air. And the plain before me was so vast that these people would emerge every second or two, as if they were marking time on a clock. Closing the window, I sank exhausted to the featherbed and wrapped myself in its folds. Soon I was warm, and I began to fall in and out of sleep like a boat rocking

on the tide. Before I was pulled into the gravityless world, I stroked my forehead, and closed my eyes as if my mother and father were kneeling by my bed. All children should have parents who love them as I will love you, but those who are born to be alone can be comforted only by an impossible task. My task was certainly not easy, and at every moment it brought to me the love that I had never known.

In the morning when I left my bed and put on my yam curler's dress I was so cold that an icicle could have formed on my back. I put my arms through the rope loop and stepped into the abyss. Slowly descending through blackened air and frozen smoke, I wondered how I could capture a kingdom so vast that the royal palace was divided into provinces and the button storage rooms employed six hundred clerks.

At tables twice the length of war galleons, in a room that was so big that sometimes a shooting star would flash in one of its corners or skid upon the horizon, the yam workers were eating stacks of dangerously hot yam cakes, with smoked wild boar sausage and the syrup of the North German Hippopotamus Yam, which is too sweet for baking and far too large to be a super-miniature yam, the kind that are glazed in chocolate and popped into the mouth ten at a time. So it is squeezed for its syrup in special silver presses that don't get sticky. These were in a room next to the gymnasium and evening club for the personnel of the yam research library and laboratories. I passed there once.

Breakfast was good. We brushed our teeth at long alabaster sinks with mango and pineapple motifs on the faucet handles, suggesting that once the yam kitchen had been attached to the realm of tropical fruit.

Then I was taken to the sorting apron. In the first few weeks I came

quite close to death by boiling, chopping, frying, baking, or simply a plunge into the pit of yam-eating aahhs! Whatever they were, you could hear their squeaks echoing faintly up the 200-foot shaft. The apron was extremely slippery, and the slipperiness was not uniform. Different types of yam dust had different coefficients of friction. As you swept and cheered the yams toward the sorting gates, you could easily slip on your hip. Down you would go, sliding toward one of the deadly exits.

You had to right yourself immediately, and, if you could not, make your broom perpendicular to the shaft, and there you would dangle above the squeaks, hot oils, or automatic knives until you could crawl back to the apron.

At ten I was nimble and new enough to learn this very quickly, and soon I was doing my job effortlessly. This did not mean I was happy. Indeed, I was not. For my task was so daunting that I was haunted. Upon entering the city I had been overwhelmed by the complexity and power of the obstacles I would have to overcome were I to reach the usurper. His power came not from within, for he himself was less than nothing: his power came from the webs of things that were spun around him.

What could I do? For one, I was not allowed anywhere but the sorting area of the yam kitchen. Were I to have appeared, for example, in the frying halls, my pass would have been wrong and I would have been sent to selection.

I doubted very much that the usurper even knew of the yam kitchens, much less the sorting area. He might not even have been aware of the starch section. And if ever he even took a bite of yam, he might have mistaken it for a sweet potato. That's how expendable we were, how isolated, and how unknown. I despaired after thinking of a hundred unworkable schemes — arming the yam workers and burst-

ing through the kitchen barriers, descending from my tower onto the palace roofs and journeying through the ducts to assassinate the usurper; and others, all made impossible by the armies of guards and the guarding armies and the fact that no one I might ask knew where in the palace the royals actually lived. You could walk about for the rest of your life and not see half of it.

Not being able to do anything, I did nothing. Every day I felt as if I had sunk lower and lower, as if I had failed. As I resigned myself to my odd form of slavery, the darkness seemed impenetrable. Then came a friendly ray of light.

One bleak morning in January, long after I had been inured to growing old like Elena in the yam kitchens, she came to me at the sorting apron and called me down. She brought me over to a window, past which the snow flew in driving lines that suddenly would change course with a snap, like a dog shaking its prey.

"You've been taken from the sorting apron," she said, almost whispering, looking at me in a wondering way. "You are the first person ever to be removed from the apron before the normal passage of the five-year apprenticeship."

I had no idea what was happening.

"Perhaps you're a rhubarb spy..." she said, looking at me carefully.

"What is a rhubarb spy?" I asked.

"You're not a spy. But I don't understand. You've been instructed to move to the distant margins of the yam kitchen, to the sector near the door to the world of the bakeries. None of us has ever been there. You will be able to see through that door to the great avenues of ovens, and it is said that things happen there that we cannot even imagine."

"Why not just walk through the door and take a look?" I asked.

Elena jumped back as if I had hit her. "Child, you talk like a princess! No yam worker has ever passed into the bakery section and come back. You know not of what you speak, for the world is wider than you can conceive."

I shrugged my shoulders. Even before I had discovered who I was and whence I had come, the freedom of the mountains had taught me to believe that the world was, indeed, mine, that I was forever free, that only God could tell me my place.

"Through that door," Elena went on, "pass the yam syrups and honeys that the bakers use invisibly to give their breads and cakes a touch of art. We've been told that you are needed there to push the carts and load the pallets. Why you when we have men four times your size? How should I know? I only know what the Duke of Tookisheim tells me."

"The Duke of Tookisheim told you that?"

"Of course not. I would never be able to speak to a duke. I would never be privileged to speak to someone who had met someone who had spoken to a duke."

"Who told you then?"

"Ssshh! Don't hear. It was Astrahn and Notorincus."

"You do know them," I said. "How? They're bakers."

"Though yam workers are forbidden to trespass in the bakeries, bakers can enter the yam kitchens. They are like noblemen. And they told me. Now, go! If you're late they'll be angry."

"Astrahn and Notorincus wouldn't be angry at *me*," I said, somewhat royally.

"Young lady, Astrahn and Notorincus are our betters. You must not assume or instruct in their regard. Is that clear?"

"But Elena, Notorincus is a slave, and Astrahn is the slave of a slave. How can they be our betters?"

"Ah! You are so foolish! If you work hard all your life you may be lucky enough to become the slave of a slave. Even the slave of a slave cannot be taken to selection (unless he is caught with a watch on his person), and he can be killed only by a nobleman. We, on the other hand, well, it is assumed that we go to selection, and only our great good luck that we don't. No law says we don't. We have merely been overlooked, like a colony of insects in a beam lost deep within the palace. That is why you must hold your breath as you live, and it is why you must love the emperor and praise him, and be happy with whatever the Duke of Tookisheim tells you."

I nodded, but I turned to the window and under my breath I said, "When I get to be queen, I am going to have this duke brought before me on a *spit*, and I'll say, 'Tookisheim, I hope you have a strong heart, for you are going to make one turn over the fire for every lie that has ever been trumpeted from your fop-filled newsrooms.'"

I hadn't realized that I was no longer free, that I had to look up to the slave of a slave and bat my eyelashes like a little doll. I didn't like that. I really didn't like that, and I stomped through the yam kitchens with such anger and disgust that everyone stepped out of my way.

This usurper, who was not of royal blood, had taken my kingdom, and if I had had an immense angel with a sword behind me, as once I may have, I would have flown through the solid walls of the palace to slay him without further ado. But I had a longer road to travel than just that, and I soon found myself pushing carts of yam syrups to the door between the bakery world and the yam world in which I was trapped like a fly in a honey crock.

"Who is this little girl who is so surly?" one of the soldiers at the doorway asked as I stood, scowling, while the cart was unloaded on the other side before it was pushed back to us.

No one answered.

"I asked, who is she?" the soldier said, his hand migrating slowly to his sword.

All those around me were so terrified that they could not move. "Apologize to him," one of them whispered, "or our wives and children will be sent to selection."

Obviously, I had no choice. I dropped to one knee, bent my head, and said, "Majesty, please forgive one who is lower than the slave of a slave. I was not surly, I was speechless in awe of your greatness."

A moment passed, and the soldier smiled. "All right," he said. "I'll take only half the children to selection. The others may live."

In this moment time stood still. The mothers and fathers of the children who pushed the carts were both grateful and grieved. Their hearts broken yet again, they prepared to lose their children, and at the same time they were grateful that half would be spared.

But royal blood is royal blood. "This is a gift?" I asked, straightening, holding my head high. Even the soldier was amazed. "This is your smiling gift? That you will kill only half the children?"

I haven't the slightest idea of what I would have done next had not Astrahn and a group of slaves burst in from the bakery side. Astrahn pulled a short broadsword from within the folds of his slave tunic and killed the first soldier. Then two other soldiers drew their own swords and approached Astrahn rather contemptuously. I suppose they simply did not believe that a slave could fight, especially as odd-looking and buff-colored a creature as Astrahn. But that a slave could fight was, indeed, the last thing they ever learned.

A woman in the background began to shriek and wail that we would all die, that everyone in the yam kitchens would be slaughtered.

I was going to give my speech then. And, who knows? It might have worked, and it might not have. Probably not. They were too afraid. They wouldn't have believed me when I told them who I was. But before my first words could tumble forth, Astrahn put his hand over my mouth and pulled me back. The other slaves quickly loaded the soldiers onto carts, covered them perfectly, and gave instructions to the trembling yam workers.

"You people have a shaft at the end of which are yam-eating … what do you call them?"

"*Aahh!*" was the horrified answer.

"Whatever. Drop these gentlemen in and wash the carts. Then go back and continue as if nothing has happened."

"What about the blood?" someone asked, but the bakery slaves were already scrubbing the floors.

"Everyone be silent," Astrahn commanded. He then said something that made my heart soar and filled my eyes with a picture of the future.

"You are now sworn to the rebellion. Whether or not you would have chosen it, it is now your path."

I myself could never be sworn to the rebellion, as the oath was pledged to the rightful sovereign, who was me.

From that moment on, everything proceeded at very high speed. I was whisked away, my badge was changed, and the next thing I knew I was traveling, with Astrahn and Notorincus on either side of me, high above a great plain of bakers and their ovens. I felt as if we were flying, but we were merely riding on a bench that had been suspended from one of the overhead conveyor chains that were used to carry supplies.

"Nice to see you again," Notorincus said, bashfully of course. "Would you like to take a nap?"

"A nap?" I asked. "What will happen next?" I feared that I wouldn't know what to do, and wanted them to brief me, as fast as they could, before we had to leave the aerial bench.

"It will take five or six hours to cross the bakery floor," Astrahn said in his somewhat elevated way. "Why don't you rest for a few hours, and then we'll tell you what you must do. Nice to get some rest, no?"

I fingered my new badge. Theirs were yellow with red borders, mine purple and gold. "Yes," Astrahn said. "Ours are the highest-level bakery badges. Yours is the highest-level service badge for the royal quarters, which are many hours away."

"Why?" I asked.

"Don't worry," Notorincus said. "Though it's forged, no one can tell the difference."

"But what am I going to do?"

"Have a rest, and when you've got your strength back, we'll tell you."

As I leaned against Notorincus, I was warmed by his soft and furry pelt, and we climbed a little on the chains, always speeding forward gently. Under the roof ahead was darkness, and in the limitless open space below, the fires of a hundred thousand ovens were twinkling in the distance. Far beneath us, bakers in their remote islands and avenues moved calmly, baking and glazing, writing whole books with their pastry tubes. They didn't know that we were gliding high above them in the warm air that smelled of cakes and icing. The chain made a pleasant, old-fashioned, clinking noise, and Notorincus patted my head. "Take a nap," he said. "Have a good sleep. We'll awaken you an hour or two before we approach the bakery frontier. All will be well."

My eyes could hardly believe the gentle scene before me, or that such a roof could exist without a single column, but then I remembered that the sky, which was far greater, had not a single column either.

"Sleep," said Notorincus, and as we calmly sailed through the darkness, I did.

When I awoke I thought I was dreaming. We had risen to such a high altitude that no longer could we see the individual bakers at work on the plain below, and the fires of their ovens looked like a carpet of gold stars. The air was clear and the roof above us invisibly black. Other than a faint rush of warm wind and the occasional muted sound from the apparatus that carried us along, all was silence.

"You're up," Notorincus said.

I rubbed my eyes and yawned.

"You had a good rest. You slept for four and a half hours and you didn't stir once: your sleep was deep."

"Is it night or day?"

"We don't know. Near the frontier there are no windows to the outside, and we haven't passed a courtyard in an hour."

"Don't you have a watch?" I asked.

"Bakers use hourglasses, and if a slave is caught with a watch he is sent to selection. But Astrahn risks all. He has a watch."

"The slave of a slave has a watch?" I asked.

"I was not always the slave of a slave," Astrahn said, with such great dignity that I felt ashamed for my question.

"Before I fell into slavery I was a general of the Damavand cavalry.

After the usurper murdered the Prince of Esterhazy, we continued to serve the good emperor, but we knew the day would come when the usurper would take his place, so we prepared for war.

"The good emperor's son took the throne, but the usurper remained. Only when the son was murdered did the Damavand rise. Given the enormity of the crime, how could we not have risen?"

I choked, prepared to hold back tears.

"Somehow the good emperor's son had discovered the daughter of the Esterhazys, grown to womanhood. This was a miracle, for we all had believed that she had been killed with her mother and father. But then the usurper found them, and their child, and finished the task he had started so long before. Not only did he murder the prince and the daughter of the Esterhazys, but their newborn infant, who would have been our queen.

"Three generations of our royalty have fallen to him, and the blood of those generations is our blood."

"Do you know anything," I asked, "about the infant princess?"

"There is a legend," he answered, "that, like her mother, she escaped. There is a legend," he said, "that she lives. It is said, or it once was, that an angel stood behind her, that she was saved, and that when she returns, a fiery angel will announce her coming. If it were so, the people would rise up all at once, a great weight would be lifted, and the light of our days would come clear. But I fear that it is not so. Ten years have passed."

"And if she did return," I asked, "and the people did rise, would they be slaughtered?"

Astrahn smiled at me bitterly and wearily. He was, after all, a warrior who had become a slave. And he had sworn to conduct a rebellion that, after ten years, must have seemed impossible. How brave

he was. "If she returned," he said, with his voice full of an emotion I could not then understand, "if she returned, a hundred Damavand generals would emerge from slavery and armies would form around them like swarms of bees. The announcement that she lives would spread like lightning, and no one would sleep until the armies were gathered to strike at the usurper. But we must find another way, or be forever lost in a dream."

"What is the other way?"

"I am not high enough to know. All I can tell you is that you have been summoned to appear at a dinner for the Legates of Pomerania and the Viscounts Regent of Dolomitia-Swift."

"Summoned by whom?"

"We down here know not by whom."

"But you are a general."

"Ah, but as there are slaves of slaves, there are generals of generals."

"What am I to do at this dinner? Who will be there? Where will it take place?"

"It is a state dinner in one of the petite dining rooms: only a thousand guests will attend, but it's very important. The usurper must throw the most exquisite dinner for the viscounts, because Dolomitia-Swift is the only kingdom that is more powerful than our own. The royals, the guests of honor, and the usurper himself will sit upon the water dais, where you will refresh flowers between courses. They use small girls for this, for you must walk along tight paths on the table to place the roses and peonies. When boys do it they kick over the stemware and the usurper selects them right on the spot. He'll select you too if you do the same, but girls are more graceful. Just be careful."

"The usurper eats?"

"Yes, at a table of fifty upon the water dais, which floats in a crystal

pool over the sides of which water flows in a continuous and even fall that is lighted from within. Those who dine upon it think they are as high as the angels. And there you will be, walking delicately upon a vast table, carrying blooms to the flower stations."

I tightened my lips, and asked, "Am I to kill the usurper?"

"No!" Astrahn cried, while Notorincus shook his head to and fro like a dog shaking off water, saying "No! No! No! No!"

"Why not?" I asked.

"First of all," Astrahn said, "how would you do it?"

"I don't know. I'd hit him."

"Don't be ridiculous. He wouldn't even know you were there. And even were you able to kill him it would do us no good, as we have no sovereign. A rebellion must feed upon the hope not only of pulling down one flag, but of raising another in its place.

"And, then, it may be that *no one* can kill the usurper."

I looked at him askance.

"The usurper isn't a simple soldier, and all precautions have been taken to protect him. His cloak is of a secret metal fiber that is so light it floats and so strong that it sloughs off the bolts of the heaviest crossbow. His mask is of the same stuff, and he always wears a hat."

"His throat?"

"Protected by the cloak. He may look horrid, but he's safe. The only way to wound him would be to strike his cheeks, and this has been tried, as you will understand when you see the many scars there, but it has never sufficed to kill him."

"Astrahn, why am I being brought there?"

"Quite frankly, my dear," Astrahn replied, "I don't know. You'll have to see."

He peered ahead, and pulled a pocket watch from the folds of his tunic. It was a very beautiful, ornate, gold disk set with lighted jewels.

"How do the jewels glow?" I asked.

"Within is a tiny fire that will burn as long as it is not questioned. If you doubt it, it goes out."

"Who would doubt it?" I asked. "You can see its light with your eyes."

"There are some," Astrahn replied, "who are so pinched and checkered of soul that they stare upon it and doubt it still. Now, let's see." He held the watch away from him, as an aged person might, and read the time. "Six-twenty. The problem is, I never know if it's a.m. or p.m. I think it's evening now, and I think we should soon be coming to the frontier."

Within a minute or two of Astrahn's pronouncement we began to descend, gliding lower and lower through the darkness toward a great jewelled cliff, where the door was particularly busy with long trains of baked goods passing through, and the rest of the jewels were lighted windows in the wall of the royal reception sections. Some were like yellow sapphires, with candlelight showing through: others, dimly skylit, were like sapphires of blue. The small dining room was another hour's travel beyond the frontier, but I had begun to be nervous even before we left the conveyor. After all, I had never walked primly among stemware on a banquet table as big as a meadow.

Notorincus, who must have read my mind, said, "Don't worry, the flower girls are so good they have never kicked over a single glass. You'll see. Their skill and confidence will pass to you."

"How?"

"The music makes them certain, and encloses their every move within the golden rails of perfection. In fact, they seem to take pride in the danger, and to know that their flawless performance is a message of defiance.

"And they never fail, for if they fail, they die. There is a legend, on the flower-growing prairies of the southern roofs, that angels guide their feet."

We had come to the jewelled wall, and behind us stretched the vast darkness of the baking plain. I took a breath, and prepared to start my new career.

L eaving Astrahn and Notorincus behind, I journeyed for another hour to the heart of the royal reception region. I passed through so many an ornate chamber, so many a marbled hall, and so many a long gallery the end of which was far from sight, that I thought I might never return. In this journey I was escorted by two guides of the key, a class of people whose entire lives were spent studying the geography of the palace. All the guides of the key in the royal regions were old and crotchety, for they had been pulled in from the outer realms, where the disturbances were too great and the going sometimes too strenuous for any but the strongest youth.

"Where are we now?" I might ask.

"This is a secondary transit hall — see (they would say, pointing up), the gilding has relatively few angels — laid crosswise over the topmost tier of the Sixteenth Royal Desk Accessory Storage Structure. Structures fifteen through eighteen are for desktop items of ebony, burled walnut, alabaster, and amber. Unlike the gold, platinum, and precious stone structures, they need only rudimentary guard quarters and chapels, so the transit hall was run across the top."

"How close are we to the roof, then, if we are over the topmost tier?"

They laughed. "The roof, little yam slave with a royal pass, is *six hundred tiers above us!*"

I wanted to know what lay in those six hundred tiers.

"Would you really like us to say?" they asked, wrinkling their deathly pale faces so that their red eyes seemed to be set impossibly far back from their bladed noses. "We can tell you what is on every single tier. Shall we recite?" Powder flew from their wigs as a door ahead was opened, and their eyes flashed with sparks of vermilion light.

"No," I said, carefully. "Just tell me what is on the two hundred and twenty-eighth tier up, and the five hundred and ninety-third."

"Section four B," one said mechanically (they were totally insane), "subsection twelve, pillar seventeen, tier two hundred and twenty-eight: ladies underwear, archaic and out of fashion, silk. Tier five hundred and ninety-three: tomato fertilizer sticks, nontoxic, various lengths and thicknesses, for greenhouse use only."

Wanting to test their acuity, I asked, "Where might I find the tailor shop for the repair and maintenance of the winter clothing that used to be used by the podiatrists who were attached to the rhinoceros-horn carving apprenticeship program?"

"The African, the Asian, or the Mexican rhinoceros?" one of the key guides asked in the most disdainful way.

"Mexican rhinoceros?" was my reply. I thought I had caught them.

"Little yam slave," said the one whose wig had shed the most powder, his contempt so acidic that it burned through his teeth and tongue and twisted his face into what looked like an ancient bas-relief of a ram, "we have breeding programs: husbandry section five zero six, Seventeenth Agriculture Pavilion, fifteenth tier, Experimental Farming Tower, SW ten-forty."

"You idiots," I said. "You know everything but you know nothing. I ought to have you flayed alive for your preposterous arrogance."

This made them laugh. "Quite uppity for a girl yam slave," they twitted. "Do you realize," they continued, fingers dancing like the crazed tubes of an overstimulated sea anemone, "that either one of us, being true slaves, could have you selected for no reason whatsoever? We've passed a hundred security stations already, and as we get closer to the center they get thicker and thicker. All we have to do is bring you to one and point."

I said nothing, but a little while later the air grew so sweet that I knew we were near the honey vats. And when we raced along a catwalk above a lake of waxen honey, the kind used in royal chocolates, I urged them to peer over the rail.

"Why?" they asked.

"To see a special substructure in the honey vats that no key guide knows, but that even non-slaves in the yam kitchen sing of in their lullabies."

"That's impossible! The honey vats have no substructures. The plum cordial vats have twenty-eight substructures, but that is due to the low viscosity of plum liqueur. The honey vats were built for an average viscosity of seven point two. They have no substructures."

"Right down there," I said. "I see them."

They leaned over to look, and as they did I bent, grasped an ankle of each one, and quickly stood up. Their hairpin legs became the levers that catapulted them over the rails. I watched them spin and tumble, and after they landed in the honey they shook their fists in rage, but I heard nothing of what they said, because they were too distant. They had quite a long swim ahead of them, as even the best swimmers cannot move through honey with prodigious speed.

I was lost, but I didn't feel lost, and I kept walking, taking turns here and there where I thought it might be appropriate. I felt as if, truly, the palace were mine and I had been in it many times before. I think this was my father speaking through my blood. He has done this so many times since, and he had done it, even without my knowledge, so many times before, that I am sure of it.

Though I never knew my father, his early touch taught me to rule, and though I took my mother's milk only for a short time, she has breathed into my lungs the clouds that float above the Damavand highlands, and the songs of the Veil of Snows. To them I owe all, and this I knew even then.

In crisp order I pre-positioned myself at the door of the flower girls, off the service ramp that led in a shell-like spiral up to the center of the water dais. I adjusted my yam curling dress, cleared my throat, and knocked.

The old man who received me was the flower master of the royal table, a Damavand to his toes. I announced that I had come from the yam kitchens.

"How did you get here without a key guide?" he asked in astonishment.

"I knew the way."

He looked at me as if to look through me, and then shook his head. Ignoring the thought that probably had shot through him like the momentary light of a distant summer storm, he said, "You were assigned key guides at the frontier. What happened to them?"

"Well," I said, "if in their curriculum the key guides do not give short shrift to swimming, they will eventually resume their profes-

sion. Otherwise, at some time in the far future when the honey vats are excavated for renovation two key guides will be memorialized in one of the many palace museums, perhaps next to dinosaurs in blobs of amber."

"Ah," he said. "You came *that* way." I don't think he knew what to make of me, as I had begun to speak with a pronounced royal twist.

"Yes," I answered. "And, by the way, I think that in the future I will decree that a middle light be placed between the red and green lanterns of traffic signals. It will be amber, to warn of one's fate if one ignores the change from green to red."

The flower master narrowed his eyes. "You are a crazy little girl," he said. "You talk like a queen." He looked about to see if we were within anyone's earshot. "Your badge is forged, and it can be detected. Don't call attention to yourself by talking like royalty. I don't know why, but the high generals summoned you here, and in less than half an hour you'll begin to refresh the flowers at the royal table as the banquet begins.

"Let me take you to the flower girls. They'll show you, on a mock-up of the table, exactly how to place bunches of peonies in the flower station between the Duke of Tookisheim and the Second Viscount of Dolomitia-Swift.

"Be careful. Your life depends upon it." And then, though not to me or to anyone in particular, he said, "I do not understand the high command. I simply do not understand them."

I was shocked to find myself suddenly among the flower girls, whose dress and footwear were more splendid than anything I had ever seen, and they were more amazed than I when I took to

those clothes as easily as if I had been born in them. And though I was neither the oldest nor the tallest, I seemed to tower over the others. I exchanged my yam curler's dress for a blue silk that was achingly beautiful even in comparison with the other flower girls' rather splendid wardrobe. It had been provided for me, I was told, but no one knew by whom. I began to suspect that the Damavand generals in slavery had gotten wind of my presence. How else to explain the provision of this truly royal dress, and my sudden assumption from the yam kitchens to the water dais? I was wrong. The Damavand generals hadn't a clue that I was in the city or even that I was alive. But things seemed to be moving, if only by magic, and I did not want to stand in the way of my good luck.

As we waited, we gossiped, although I had nothing to gossip about and knew none of the noble names that were flipped through the air like darts. I had taken my instruction from a little girl who, despite her absolute surety of foot, stuttered like an off-center mill wheel. I went over her directions again and again, not only to be sure of them, but because she spoke in multiple copies.

Pay no attention to the nobles. Ignore their conversation, which is idiotic, and listen only to the music. The music will make you feel as if the table is your garden and you are a princess happily taking flowers from it in bright sunshine. Walk gracefully, proudly, as if you were a noble yourself, as if the world were perfect.

At eight exactly, by the high-precision cuckoo clock in the hall where we waited, the music began. It would take half an hour for the nobles to assume their places, and then an equal amount of time for the royals to make their entrances and mount the water dais. Only after all were assembled would the usurper and his rock-cold queen ascend to their thrones at table, amidst cheers and applause from the

nobles they fed, like dogs, with bits of gold and snippets of position. I vowed that when and if I became queen I would never indulge in such ritual, and I have not.

Though agitated, I was not afraid, and even had I been, the music would have given me courage, for music is the magical organizer of chaos, its presence a sure reminder that even the blackest darkness rests upon sparkling trusses of pure light, and by the time the usurper had been seated and the serving begun, I was ready to fly into any kind of battle and meet any kind of test. Then we were signaled by the flower master, and with our arms full of flowers we climbed the spiral stairs that led to an opening in the forest centerpiece, and we spilled out along our assigned pathways on the linen.

Laden with peonies, I walked slowly toward my station between the Second Viscount of Dolomitia-Swift and the Duke of Tookisheim. I curtsied, and fixed my gaze upon the blooms that were already there, waiting for one to wilt. Though my obligation was to keep my eyes riveted upon the flowers, this was my palace, my hall, and my table, so I looked about as I pleased. No one noticed. They were too absorbed in the music, their own conversation, and the dangers of placing a huge set of nobleman's buttocks upon a small velvet chair (had these chairs been of appropriate size, it would have been insulting). The dinner guests had arrived in upper-body masks, giraffe heads, cockatoo coats, and other oddities that, after their entrance, most entrusted to a mask-check girl. Others did not. Why do the very rich love to dress as birds, stingrays, Mandarins, giraffes, pirates, and Nubian dancers? Can it be genetic? I have never found it anything but horrifying, and I have half a mind to abolish it.

I did not see the usurper at first, for though this was my hall, my table, and my palace, and though I had seen him before, I was hesi-

tant to look closely upon the face of this man who had taken so much from me, my kingdom being the smallest part of it. When, in moving my eyes ever so cautiously, I locked them upon his repellent form, I saw there the marriage of power and evil.

Do not dismiss those who stand above you, for very seldom are they there by chance. Most often their power is genuine, their evil a power in itself, and their visage impressive. The usurper's face was many times the size of mine, and seemed even larger than it was. His smile was fixed, revealing huge teeth and immense incisors. He looked as if he might eat you, like a wild animal, and the plains of his cheeks resembled a battle helmet. Upon these plains were the scars of crossbow bolts, arrows, and knives, their presence a testament to his invulnerability.

You could see in his eyes that, if indeed he had a soul, it was someplace else, but that he was enjoying the dinner nonetheless, even if he enjoyed it not at all. He lived for absolute power, and his possession of it was confirmed in ceremony after ceremony, dinner after dinner, by the strength of his armies and the slavish obedience of his flacks. I had seen the selections. My own family had been among the first. This and my destiny kept me the model of girlish grace, smiling and light on my feet as I held my post. I turned my eyes from the usurper, determined to meet them one day, close and clear, in the presence of death. And from this I took a certain joy.

With no flowers wilting and nothing for me to do, I was able to turn my attention to the conversation. The Duke of Tookisheim, a snakelike cross between a ninny and a fop, was hectoring Peanut, who sat next to him in a raspberry-colored coat. The Duke totally ignored the Viscount of Dolomitia-Swift on his other side, because he was, apparently, incensed at Peanut's coiffure.

"Peanut, where did you have your hair done?" he asked.

"I didn't. I just took a shower and combed it out. Or, rather, I had a Pretzelian slave boy comb it out."

"How many times have I told you," the Duke said, "that Tookisheims take care of their hair? Look at mine. Do you know how many hours a day I spend on it?"

"I'm the one who runs the papers," Peanut said, holding a spoon like a knife pointed at his father, "and I didn't have time. Besides, my hair's different from yours. It's black. It already has gray in it. I have mother's hair. I prefer it. All your flounces make you look like a twit."

"You'll hear from me, Peanut!" the Duke of Tookisheim said. "You'll hear from me!" He was vibrating with rage, and all this was said in front of me, as if I were a statue, and would neither hear nor remember.

When the Duke was finished with Peanut, he produced a blizzard of compliments aimed at the usurper, and then, as his sycophancy grew flat he changed the tone to one of frustrated commiseration. "Sire," he said, "your reforms make much sense, but the people are selfish and their resistance maddening."

"The people need to be shown what is good for them, Tookisheim," the usurper said in a voice so deep that the stemware rattled.

"Yes, sire. You are a brilliant leader, and capable of convincing anyone of virtually anything, but the people are hoodwinked by the selfish Damavand generals hidden among the slaves. They spread the doctrine of self-interest, and they lie with impunity."

"And they must be destroyed," the usurper said, going into a funk.

"Come now, Tookisheim, old chap," said the Second Viscount of Dolomitia-Swift, in a voice that froze me in shock, "is it really so selfish for a person to attend to his own interests? Isn't that the stated purpose of the reforms, to serve all these people whom you call selfish?"

"Ah," said Tookisheim. "The point is, Viscount my boy, that laborers, petty merchants, and small farmers can't know what serves them best. They're always deluded and greedy. They think that if they are happy, all are happy, and they do not know that only if all are happy can they be happy. My task is to educate them, to lift them beyond their selfishness, to show them that each and every one of them must be willing to sacrifice himself for the good of all of them."

"But Tookisheim, old chap," the Second Viscount said, "consider the case of the paper makers of the Hoggenstrasse. They are taxed to death solely that they may enjoy the benefit of things such as the royal amputation wagons and compulsory tattoos. They don't want these things, and would be happier deciding how to use the fruits of their labor without interference. After all, you do."

"Yes," said Tookisheim. "But I'm *educated*. I don't live in a tiny little house. I don't lust after cheap bicycles and funny-looking clothes. What is the purpose of the elite if not to correct the misguided?"

"You may not lust after cheap bicycles, Tookisheim old chap, but you *are* covered in flounces, you have ribbons on your shoes, and you have enclosed your bulk in a sickening swamp-green coat."

"Naturally," the Duke of Tookisheim said, forgetting that he had checked his mask. "I'm a giraffe."

"Ah, but Tookisheim, a giraffe's brain is so much bigger."

"I beg your pardon!" said the Duke of Tookisheim. "How is it, anyway, that you presume to comment on the affairs of the kingdom, having arrived only this morning from Dolomitia-Swift, a place known to be strictly *bourgeois*."

"Don't be offended, old fellow," the Second Viscount of Dolomitia-Swift said with a cheerfulness that made the usurper boil. "Because we in Dolomitia-Swift desire friendly relations, we have made a careful

study of your kingdom. Much is lacking, Tookisheim dear chap, and the heart of it is that you cannot rule in the name of your people if you imagine that it is your place to instruct them. You see, Tookisheim old fellow, in Dolomitia-Swift we learned long ago that when the power of government is married with the urge to instruct, it produces the bastard of coercion. And it doesn't matter what your motives are."

"This has gone beyond the bounds!" the usurper said, and, upon hearing his voice, a thousand people moved to the edges of their little velvet seats. Even the waiters, usually models of discretion, stood pop eyed and open mouthed, their trays of caviar-stuffed road hen stilled in air. "I remind the Second Viscount of Dolomitia-Swift," the usurper growled in a tone so low that it was undoubtedly memorialized by the palace seismographs, "that my armies are overflowing with vigor and wanting of activity."

To this the Second Viscount responded, "Well said, Emperor. I receive your comments with all humility, and will be sure to repeat them to the generals of Dolomitia-Swift, whose armies, as you know, are, have always been, and will always remain … *invincible.*"

This galled the usurper, who knew that, in fact, the armies of Dolomitia-Swift were preternaturally invincible. Here the Duke of Tookisheim saw an opening, yet another opportunity to serve the usurper. "Why don't you shut up, you fat thing!" he shouted at the viscount.

The viscount laughed, and although I had not surely known him by his voice, I did know him by his laugh, and I trembled with joy that he had broken his vow. "Tookisheim, dear fellow," the viscount said, "I'm not fat. You are the one who is fat." And indeed, Tookisheim was whalish, elephantine, and porcine, although not necessarily in that order, whereas, even at an advanced age, the viscount was still trim.

"I'm going to have a section of the *Tookisheim Post* on how bad it is to

make fun of fat people!" the Duke of Tookisheim shouted, shaking his finger at the viscount. "I'll have ten sections! And every day I'll have eight or nine articles — interviews with fat people whose feelings have been hurt, fat people who can't be in the Olympics, experts who tell us why we are so cruel, and why it's bad to be thin. I'll invent a new name for fat people. I'll call them hefty. I'll call them chunky. I'll call them beefy. No, I'll call them . . . muscular!" At this, the table exploded in laughter — even the usurper. And when the Duke of Tookisheim saw the usurper laughing at him, he laughed at himself, and was happy.

During this distraction, the viscount leaned forward and whispered to me. "My Queen," he said. "My dear Queen. How glad I am to see you, and thanks be to God that you are safe." And then, just before attention had begun to shift back to him, he quickly said, "Climb to the great clock before sunrise. You will find me in its workings."

This Viscount of Dolomitia-Swift was the man I had known since birth, he who had raised me as a daughter, who had taught me everything I knew. I was overjoyed to see him, but, as he had instructed me so long before, I could not reveal myself, and I had to hold back my tears. He had brought home all the long and sad history of the kingdom and broken my heart a dozen ways when he had addressed me as he did, for never before had he called me anything but *child*, or *daughter*, and, once again, with but two words, he had sung the song of my life.

I was so happy to see the tutor that I was not paying sufficient attention, and with my right foot I knocked over the Duke of Tookisheim's seltzer glass. The seltzer shot onto his plate and picked up a lot of beet juice, which then traveled with it in wonderful de-

flection until it stopped in the Duke of Tookisheim's face and fizzed down his cravat. The Duke of Tookisheim was now beet-colored in rage, or perhaps not in rage. Red bubbles made his eyebrows supernatural, and in any case he couldn't talk.

No one laughed. Except me. I laughed. After all, it was funny, and I was the queen. I admit that my royal demeanor was inappropriate to my situation, but it was so strong within me that I was unable to suppress it. My laughter was the only sound in the dining room, where you could have heard a flea dropping its diaper pin. And then, in the silence that followed, that flea's breathing would have sounded like the roar of the falls that plummet from the slopes of Mount Dalkash.

The usurper lifted his finger and motioned for me to approach. Though no one else was breathing, I was not afraid. I no longer knew how to be afraid, for I was the queen, and I trusted in my divine right.

I looked this man in the eyes, this man who had killed my mother and father, and I broke him. No one in attendance understood what had happened, not even he, not even I. But now I know. He could have killed me instantly in any of a hundred ways, and the witnesses would not have moved a muscle or even spoken of it after dinner. I was at his mercy. I had no power. I had no armies. I had nothing. But I was in the right, and I did not flinch.

Nor, might I add, did he. We stared eye to eye. "What," he asked, in his booming voice — ah, the exhalations of pure fear that filled the hall! — "is so funny?"

I answered, like a queen, directly. "The Duke of Tookisheim has beet juice all over him, and he looks like an idiot. That's because he is an idiot."

At once Peanut Tookisheim jumped up. "My father is not an idiot!" he shouted.

"Shut up!" the usurper bellowed, the ice of his soul already beginning to shatter.

"Shut up!" Peanut Tookisheim said to himself, and sat down.

"You," the usurper said, pointing his finger at me from a clenched fist. "You . . ." It seemed very likely that he was going to kill me. What held him back was that I was tranquil, embraced by the bonds of providence.

In a defiant whisper, I asked, "What about me?"

How I tempted fate in those days when I was young. The usurper was about to dispatch me when the Second Viscount of Dolomitia-Swift rose from his seat and fearlessly, almost casually, addressed him in front of all. "As the child has been in my service at this meal, it will be an intolerable affront to my honor if she is harmed. Nay, if she is *inconvenienced*. The invincible armies of Dolomitia-Swift will strike your kingdom like a steel hammer upon eggshell. A diplomat must be treated with proper respect. It is the law of nations, and Dolomitia-Swift stands at the ready right now to prove my words. The decision, Emperor, is yours."

Of course, that was not so, as the real legate of Dolomitia-Swift was at that moment semi-imprisoned, playing an infinite number of backgammon games with Notorincus, who never won. Nonetheless, all was at stake, and a clock high on the wall ticked like a heart out of control. After much thought, the usurper turned to Peanut Tookisheim.

"Peanut Tookisheim!" he shouted. "You will receive fifty lashes, in public, on Saturday next, and everyone in the kingdom will rejoice. Not least I."

"What for, Majesty?" asked Peanut.

"For being a nitwit," the usurper growled.

161

In this instant I was whisked away by the flower master with such speed that I felt like a mail sack pulled into a speeding train. All the flower girls were running as fast as they could, and in the incredible panic in the halls underneath the water dais the flower master and I passed them. "You must hide for the rest of your life in the deepest recesses of the kingdom," he said.

"Not quite yet," I announced. "I have an appointment."

I can see the clock tower at this very moment, in the distance over the snow-covered roofs, standing higher than any building in the city. On this bright morning with a sky as blue as the ocean, it is crowned with white, and the winds aloft are playing with the snow upon its gables and cornices just as they do on the breathless ledges of the highest mountains.

After I had slipped through the bars at the base, I climbed in the cold and darkness up its many flights of stone steps. The windows gave out upon miasmas of ice and frozen fog, and if I reached to steady myself when rounding a turn I would quickly have to pull my hand from the stone lest the two be joined by cold. With every exhausting step in the freezing darkness I found a portion of despair, for it seemed that no matter how far I had come the kingdom was too massive to go any but the way of someone like the usurper.

Yes, the tutor had arrived, and he had worked his magic, bringing me from the depths to the heights, but what did this have to do with justice or vengeance? As long as the usurper had left the hall to cheers and I was obliged to hide, the tutor's wit and magic would be of no avail.

Still, I kept rising in the tower, wanting to see him, pushing the

darkness ahead of me like a boat plowing through the night sea. It was my obligation and my desire, and eventually I came to the top of the stairs, where I turned the handle of a great door and it glided open in complete silence.

There before me, after all the darkness I had come through, was the kingdom's most wonderful room. I stepped in, closed the door, removed my heavy coat, and stood for a moment, forgetting why I had come, overwhelmed by pure observation.

I was as high above the ground as if I had been flying, as elevated as if on a summit in the first line of mountains, and yet I was in a vast room at the base of thirty stories of gleaming machinery that turned the hands of the four clock faces.

That which was not brass was gold; that not nickel, silver; that not glass, diamond or sapphire. The motive power for this machine, as the tutor had explained in what now seemed like the world before the world, was most extraordinary. A circular chain of platinum rods was draped over a geared wheel, all of gold, the size of a barn. Where the links of the chain were joined, a huge jewel the size of a melon was held in a mount. When the light of an electric arc pulsed through a battery of gems above and struck the jewels on the chain, the chain moved. The sequence had to be correct — sapphire to sapphire, diamond to diamond, emerald to emerald, and so on — but each burst of light pushed the jewels of the chain in a waterwheel of light.

As it moved, it generated the electricity that turned it, with much power left over. This, the tutor had said, was a perpetual motion machine, which, it was widely believed, could not exist. "But," he told me, and I remember this as if it were ten minutes ago, "the whole universe is a perpetual motion machine, which is to say that the original push was inexplicable except as evidence of divine splendor. So, if the entire universe is one of these machines that supposedly cannot exist, and we are in fact living inside it, why not have another?"

"Because only God is capable of building it," I answered, "not man."

"Right," the tutor said. "That we ourselves cannot build it goes without saying. That He can build it also goes without saying. It's all very simple. Yes?"

"Yes."

"Well, when we wanted another one, we asked for it."

"You did?"

"It took someone far wiser than I, but it worked."

"You mean, you asked God for a perpetual motion machine to power the clock, and it just appeared?"

"He sent it. At first He put it in the wrong place, but we revised our request and He moved it to the top of the tower."

I had never heard of such a thing, and I told him so.

"Why is it so hard to believe?" he asked. "He set up the universe, the sun, the galaxies, physical laws, and all that. Why not a clock?"

"That's wonderful," I said.

"I know," the tutor had answered.

There I stood, in a room that needed no guards, where human passion was modulated as if by magic, where the air was perfect, and the light sublime. I asked myself, who am I? A yam slave (not even a true slave), or the queen of the kingdom? And in this room the answer was absolutely clear that I was both, and that they were the same. And I asked myself, am I ten years of age or a newborn child or an old woman soon to die? And in this room the answer was the same. I was all, and none was different, not in this room. And I asked myself, can I feel pain? And the answer was, no, not in this room.

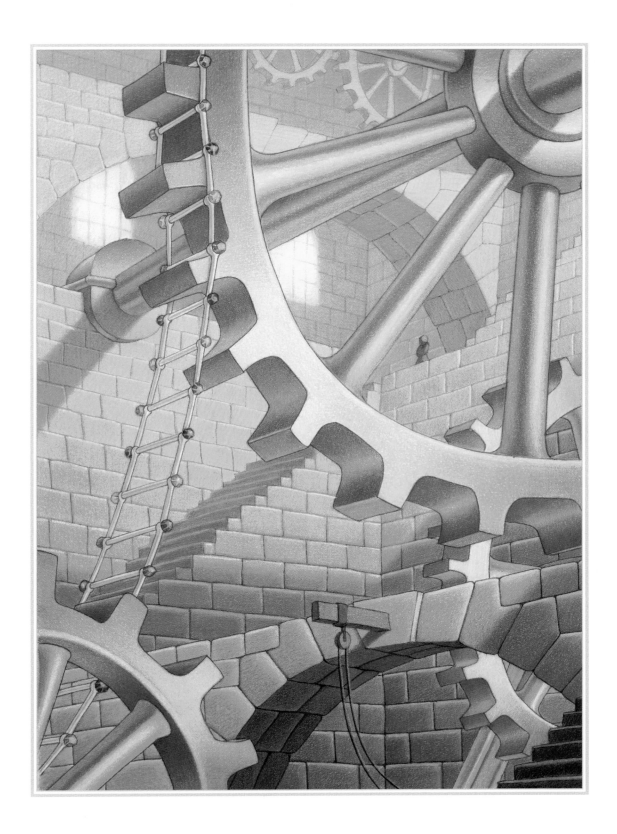

I thought of the child beneath her dying mother and father, and I thought of the child spirited across the mountains after her mother and father had sacrificed themselves so that she might live, and these thoughts that at most times I could not bear I was able to bear quite easily, in this room, for here all connections came clear, there was no longing, there was no lack. In this room perfection drove the clockwork, and its spilling over, its wonderful excess, like water tumbling over a weir, like the blast of sunlight at dawn, made everything come right. It was here that I understood that I need not grieve for those who are lost, for here I joined them.

As I walked amid the sometimes surprising flashes and sparkles of light in every color, and as the wheels turned and the darkness above sang with the progress of golden escapements, I remembered why I had come. "Tutor!" I called out. "Tutor!"

In this immense and perfect room, where would he be? I stopped to think, and the answer came. He would be in a place from which he might look out upon the imperfect world. It would have to be along the walls. And in the walls the windows or balconies would, for reasons of symmetry, be in the center. I went to the wall that faced the palace square, and at the center, far above the floor of the clock room, reached by many flights of stairs, was a door that led to a balcony. There, facing away from me, was the tutor, looking across the kingdom, backlit by rose-colored light from below.

Though up there we were enclosed in cloud and fog, and he looked like a man standing in front of a dense waterfall, I knew that his memory allowed him to survey the kingdom through the barriers that now obscured it, and that this was what he was doing. Somehow, he knew I was there, so he turned. The minute I saw his face, I ran to him, and he took me in his arms. For queen or not, blood or not, I was his child.

In the long telling of what had happened to me I discovered that, in choosing word by word what to say, I grew up. Yes, it was early, and it was magical, but often it is with kings and queens, as you yourself may discover. In summarizing to the tutor my course through the kingdom I had inherited and not yet claimed, I found that the important things rose as if under their own power, and that my tale was, surprisingly, one of equanimity and affection.

"I understand this," he said. "As you know, I have had occasion to look back myself."

"Why is it," I asked, "that some things now seem lovely and just that not long ago were so forbidding?"

"My dear Queen, for the teller of the tale, gratitude, love, and hope remain, because no matter what the story, its teller lives."

"Is that all?"

"No. It is also your duty to look with a loving eye upon all you have been given. This is what you have done, and you have done well."

I bowed my head and briefly closed my eyes. The tutor smiled, for he knew, though I did not, that this is how a queen acknowledges what is required of her.

"More to the point," he continued, "is what is to come. Events are unfreezing, and things are rising upon the wind."

"What events?" I asked. "Nothing here changes but for the worse. What can be done?"

"What must be done," he replied, "is to lead the Damavand generals from slavery and hiding. When they emerge en masse even with their ill-equipped and half-trained troops, they will be a match for the usurper's armies, and if they survive the first battles, they will triumph."

"Why haven't they done this before?" I asked. "They're only getting older."

"They cannot emerge until they have a leader, and a leader has not arisen among them. Of leaders you will find two kinds — those who choose themselves and those who are chosen. Whereas the first cannot but fail all tests after they come to power, the chosen strengthen from crisis to crisis. The paradox of the Damavand generals is that were any one to lead the others from slavery he would weaken, for the very act of proffering himself would be his demise.

"The Damavand," he said, "have been waiting for their chosen leader. They have been waiting ... for you."

"For me?"

"This, my dear Queen, is the profession of a queen."

"But I have done nothing," I protested.

"Precisely," he continued. "You are the only one fit to lead, for you have been born to it, and it is a responsibility that you must bear rather than the prize you seek. The usurper stole your throne, and he cannot rule justly. You, on the other hand, having been lifted there gently, reluctantly, are still in possession of heart, humility, and justice."

"But I'm ten years old," I said. "How am I to lead generals from slavery?"

"Though the first steps will take your breath away," he told me, "they will not be difficult. Only subsequently, in the wars that follow, when the task of commanding the armies falls upon you, and you find the great Damavand generals hanging on your every word, will it be truly difficult. But I have faith in you: I know you will succeed."

"What are the first steps?" I asked.

He turned to look at the clouds of ferociously blowing snow, rose-colored from the fires below, with edges of gold and sparklings of diamond.

"Pray that it clears," he said. "For all will be lost if, two days from now, the sky is obscured by cloud."

"Upon this the kingdom rests?"

"Kingdoms rest upon lesser things and far more unlikely than just a clear day. Kingdoms are like the life of a man. No matter how vigorous they may seem, they hang by threads. Know this for the time that will come when you have cut the usurper's threads and hang by your own."

"What of the clear day?" I asked, wanting to hear.

The tutor nodded his head slowly, as if he were hoping. "The scholars of the kingdom will receive a signal, doubly confirmed, that you are alive and that you have returned."

"How will that be?" I asked. "The usurper controls all schedules, movement, and communication. Because he spreads rumors to cloud the truth, nothing can be believed. Do you know that I have heard that my father was a devil, that when he died he became a bird? That my mother died in the city, upon the lake, in the mountains, among the clouds?"

"A way exists to cut through all that. I designed it before I left. I passed it to the scholars, of whom, in my way, I was one, for it is their job, by definition, to seek and serve the truth."

"No longer," I told him. After all, he had just arrived, and I had been in the city for what seemed like years. "They serve the usurper now, and are in league with the Duke of Tookisheim. They have become flatterers and liars and fools. The usurper emptied half the asylums and scattered the inmates throughout the universities like chocolate chips."

"Really," he said.

"Yes."

172

"But, you see," he continued, "this business of being a scholar goes back quite a long way. Its root is very deep, and it may have more life than you think. I am sure that many real scholars are left and that new ones will be created by the very process of their search for truth, and that they will shrug off the flattery and coercion of the Duke of Tookisheim and the usurper as a deer shrugs off the rain — with a little flick.

"They will know what to look for and how to read it, and when. They will inform the Damavand generals, who will gather in the palace square when the time is right. On that day the market will be more crowded than ever before. If the usurper is told of this he will delight at the strength of the economy. But!"

"But what?" I asked.

"In the square will be a thousand Damavand generals, each with a troop of a thousand dismounted cavalry. Multiply, my Queen, to see how many of your soldiers will be gathered to hear your first command."

"A million," I said, unable even to imagine such a sight.

"A million," he confirmed.

"But only a few hundred Damavand generals were taken into slavery."

"They were instructed that upon the loss of the kingdom they should tend to their numbers for the day that would come, and they have. In slavery and in exile, they have restored themselves to their original strength. They lack only practice and complete armament."

"Who gave those instructions?"

"I did, on your behalf. I had the emperor's seal. Not that overwrought diamond-encrusted serpent thing the usurper uses," the tutor said, "but the original imperial seal. Even those who have never

173

seen or heard of it, when they look upon it, understand what it is. It's right here," he said, lifting up his leather satchel and removing the seal. "It belongs to no one but you."

The beauty of the seal was overwhelming. Three dolphins arched over an agitated sea on an oval of gold crowned by a crown. I looked above to see if a light were shining upon it and saw none, which was a surprise, for the seal sparkled as if in bright sun.

"It has been near you all your life. I kept it under a plank beneath your bed. It was your grandfather's, and his father's, and his father's father's, all the way back. Your father held it for a very short time, and looked at it as if it would not be his. I was there when he received it. I saw. Now you must take it without further thought, for it will be yours as long as you live."

I took it. "Will I use this, then, to prove myself to the Damavand generals in the palace square?"

"No. The power flows from you to the seal, not vice versa. You are the sovereign, not it. You must appear on the south balcony at the midpoint of the square, the one your grandfather used, and announce yourself."

"How will I be heard? My voice is small."

"Your voice will thunder, for they will be awaiting you. When you stand before them, the kingdom will electrify and your voice will carry to its remotest corners, never mind the square, which will shake as if beaten by bolts of lightning."

I could hardly believe this. "But when will I appear?" I asked.

"You will know to assume your destiny when the most humble and unlikely person in the kingdom understands as clearly as you and I what great things will occur, when all is drama, and you feel the moment flooding through your hands like the waters of a swollen thrashing stream."

Then I took leave of the tutor, the only father I had ever known. I assumed that he would be there on the great day of which he spoke, and that he would remain by my side thereafter, to guide me in the world he knew so much better than I.

He had said goodbye almost casually, though he had made his plans so long before that he must have worried that many of the people upon whom he depended would be dead. Though many were, and many shortly would be, quite a few remained, and they were devoted.

Just as the Damavand generals had been instructed to keep their armies in the shadows, the scholars had been told, cryptically, that my return would be heralded by "a flaming angel from a dimming sun." For years, as scholars will, they debated the meaning of this phrase. Those who believed it literally became fewer and fewer. As time passed and an angel did not fall and the sun did not dim they were ridiculed, and they could not help but doubt themselves. In great tests, one always does: that is the test.

During the wars, and after, I was able to speak to them, and was not surprised to hear that, almost one and all, they had suspected that they were wrong, but they had believed nonetheless. The world of fact and event had seemed to conspire against them, for they had staked their hearts on miracles, and miracles were not forthcoming.

"Your Majesty," I was told, "I questioned my own faith so strongly that I despised myself for still believing, and, yet, I could not cease to believe, and I knew I would hold to my great expectation even on my dying day. I was prepared to go without the society of men and die alone, for everything in me said that God had spared the children, and that you would come back to us.

"My friends said, 'That is insanity,' and I answered, 'So it is, but it is also love, from which I will not stand down.' And, your Majesty, I gave up my life for this belief, not for any reward, but because of its beauty and its consistency."

Few were left to endure the discomforts of faith unproven and dreams unrealized. Nonetheless, when the day came, the few that were left were enough.

I did not think to question Astrahn and Notorincus when, after another long nocturnal flight under the limitless roof of the bakeries, they left me in the yam kitchens and rushed away. Though not until later was I to know where they were needed, I assumed that they had important business.

I was returned to the sorting apron as if in a dream, there to ponder which of my lives was real and which not. Had I been at the usurper's table? Had the tutor appeared? Had I ever lived in the South Mountains? Was I a queen? Was my parents' history what I believed? Or had I been working upon this apron for an eternity of madness and delusion?

The more time passed and the past receded, the more I lost faith, for in the end it is always the smallest things that can be grasped or proved that usurp our trust and focus our hearts — unless, by stubbornness and courage, we overcome them.

The days fled as one and none. I did not know if the air was clear or cloudy, and my heart sank when everything remained the same. For a week or two, and then a month, and longer, my hope remained alive. But then I bent my head, and my heart slept.

Unbeknownst to us as we labored in darkness, the sky had opened and the world was set in the sharp crystal that comes

176

after a blizzard. The lake, I am told, was a royal blue ribbon, with waves that rose on high winds, and swift breeze-lines of foam. From the towers and pinnacles of city and palace the white rims of the mountains were scalloped in gold as the sun moved behind them and the gales blew the snow.

Astrahn and Notorincus had been summoned posthaste to a tannery in the poorest, most ferocious part of the city, the quarter where the usurper allowed criminals to take refuge as part of his design to keep the kingdom in a state of terror. He tolerated their outrages not from any sense of idiotic mercy but because, in truth, they were involved in the same enterprise and they had the same aim. The criminals viewed the mass of people as a herd to be culled, controlled, and coerced, and in this they were the usurper's natural allies.

Even Astrahn, a Damavand general who had fought the Golden Horde, feared this place and kept his hand upon the hilt of his sword. Needless to say, Notorincus, master baker and king of the Alpine Chocolate Truffle Brioche, who never had been a soldier and was almost as round as a cinnamon roll, trembled in fear.

On the worst hill of this unspeakable quarter, in its worst hollow, and on its worst street, sat the tannery, sunk in an unbearable smell. Here, slaves who were too repulsive to bring to the executioners labored at reducing carcasses and fats, and cured the hides and skins of skunks, weasels, and toads for the belts, wallets, and hats of the criminals who strutted about the quarter. Criminals then were fond of wearing hats of skunk fur, and not one wanted to be caught dead — as sometimes they were — without a toad-skin vest.

Disappearing among the fetid vats and retching as they picked their way over soft slimy floors, Astrahn and Notorincus were led to

a tiny filth-encrusted hole in a back wall. A tannery slave pointed to it and said, "In there."

"In where?" Astrahn said, thinking of his clean tunic.

"In that hole you go."

"In that hole?"

"Yes. They all do."

"They do, do they?"

"Yes."

"And how is my friend here going to accomplish such a thing?"

The tannery slave looked over at Notorincus. "If bakery slaves suck in their stomachs and blowout all the air in their lungs we can push them through if we put some slime on the edges of the hole. We've done it before."

"But why should we go in there?" Notorincus asked.

"I don't know," the slave said. "You told us the password. People like you come here and tell us the password, and then they go in the hole."

"They do?"

"Every day. Sometimes a hundred a day. The hole used to be much smaller."

"What's in there?" Astrahn asked.

The slave shrugged his shoulders. "All I know is what the Duke of Tookisheim tells me."

This was the kingdom's most common expression, though young people had begun to say, "All I know is what Peanut Tookisheim tells me." Peanut was slowly taking charge of the *Tookisheim Post*, and his first act had been to search out anyone who knew anything and kill him. Peanut's ambition was to be even stupider than his father, and, miraculously, he was succeeding.

"I think," Astrahn told Notorincus, "that we should wait until somebody comes out, and then we'll ask what's in there."

"No one ever comes out," the slave announced matter-of-factly.

"Really," Astrahn said.

"Never. Never happened."

Both Astrahn and Notorincus stared at the hole. "Well," said Astrahn, "we have our orders. Good bye, Notorincus."

"Good bye, Astrahn."

"You go first."

"No, you go first, you're thinner."

"You'll need me to push you."

"You were a soldier. I'm just a baker."

Astrahn cleared his throat and looked archly at Notorincus. "Feet first or head first?"

Ten minutes later, after a ride at tremendous speeds along the perfectly smooth course of a river of hot mineral water, Astrahn and Notorincus, who had been unable to utter a word but had managed to grab one another's clothing, found themselves plummeting over a fall.

When they surfaced they were in an underground lake, and coming toward them over its steaming waters was a trim rosewood boat rowed by four Damavand soldiers. Standing in the prow, with a boat hook, was a Damavand lieutenant. Astrahn could hardly believe his eyes, for they were in full uniform, and the colors and emblems they wore without a thought were those he had not seen since the fall of the kingdom.

Even as he still floated, his hope and pride flooded back. "I am Astrahn," he said, "general of the First Corps of the Fifteenth Wave of Damavand cavalry." When the lieutenant dropped the boat hook and saluted as of old, Astrahn's heart was made young.

This was the Damavand high command, deep under the palace, a

hundred levels below the gushing mineral springs that the usurper's soldiers thought were the bottom layer, beneath the tunnels of the rats and amid the water-choked seams in the rock. Here was the heart of the rebellion, where the Damavand generals carried on their work. And of all this, the monstrous key guides had not the faintest clue.

When Astrahn was led into the presence of the commander of the armies, he saluted stiffly, but his eyes held tears, for he and the commander had served together against the Golden Horde and in the Great War That Was Lost, and Astrahn had thought he was dead.

"Astrahn," the general said. "I need not tell you how good it is to see you again.

"Sir."

"But I have orders for you that must be carried out on the instant. You are to take a detachment of five swordsmen and archers to the tower, where you will secure the entrance, the stairs, and the clock room. The regent, guardian of the sovereign queen, is there alone. It is your honor to protect him."

"The queen lives?" Astrahn asked, electrified.

"We don't know, but the regent has called for the scholars to assemble in the palace square, and they are doing so at this very moment."

Newly clothed in the uniform of a Damavand general, Astrahn took the five soldiers and Notorincus, who wore the Damavand Civilian Assistance Crest, through one of the many exits from the underground chambers. They emerged from beneath the peacock shelters near the clock tower, bumping their heads and collecting straw as they ducked from under the roofs. Mothers and children

were stunned to see soldiers who were not in black, but in the white and blue that they had thought they would never see again.

As the detachment double-timed through the winding streets to reach the tower, merchants ran to their windows and their patrons stood stock still. It was beyond hope, so far beyond hope that in the heart of each person to witness the passing of these soldiers rose the same refrain: "It cannot be. It cannot be ..."

But it was, and just before one of the last alleys opened upon the square they encountered twelve soldiers of the usurper's royal guard, who had been on their way from the square to a ceremony for the Lord Mayor of the Lake.

"What?" the commander said as he saw the Damavand soldiers in blue and white. "Is this for a play?"

The answer arrived before he or a single one of his men could unsheathe their swords or lift their crossbows. Astrahn called out the orders of old, as if ten years had passed not in the bakeries but at the margin of the Veil of Snows, in battle against the Golden Horde.

"Archers load," he said, still holding the pace, for Damavand soldiers did not need to stop to fire their arrows, having learned to do so at a gallop.

In a flash, five Mongol bows somersaulted over the backs of the soldiers and into their hands, followed by fifteen arrows, one set on each bow and two draped between the fingers ready to be set.

"Aim and release," Astrahn said with the dispassion that he had learned from a lifetime on the frontier, and five solid arrows from the Mongol bows found the hearts of five soldiers.

The others, for years astoundingly brave when they had no enemy, fumbled with their weapons in fear, for they were used to cutting down unarmed men and capturing women and children for the selections. Though the sight of their uniforms was in itself capable of freezing an untrained opponent, their years of strutting and posing had paralyzed their ability to fight. And to their credit they understood that this, the first engagement of the next great war, was theirs to lose. The arrows found their marks, and thus the war began, though for many weeks the usurper's armies would find no one to fight, even though they would search the kingdom for soldiers in blue and white.

And by the time I appeared on the balcony the usurper's armies would have stood down, thinking that only six Damavand soldiers and a bakery slave had been the cause of their fright, and that all was safe. But when a million soldiers in the palace square would throw off the maroon cloaks of slavery to meet the sun with a prairie of blue and white as far as the eye could see, the usurper's generals would swallow hard.

Astrahn's men reached the tower unseen, entered, and closed the door behind them. They set up their defensive positions at the choke points on the stairs. When this was done, Astrahn climbed to the clock room, and there he found the tutor, who was attending to a figure of an angel, a life-sized construction of straw and wood and wax, that stood on the platform at the top of the stairs that led to the balcony. Had the tutor been anyone but the regent of the realm, Astrahn would have asked about the angel, but he bowed instead.

"Your Majesty," he said.

The tutor, who would nervously glance at the thousands of scholars assembling below, and then at the figure of the angel, was not pleased. "I'm just the regent," he told Astrahn. "Save that for the queen."

"The queen lives?"

"The queen lives." The tutor was preoccupied, Astrahn later told me. He had several cans of paraffin that he would bend to check, and then he would tap the angel, and look up at the hands of the huge clock above them. Astrahn hardly took notice of this, so shocked was he to hear that the queen was alive.

"Where?" Astrahn asked.

"In the yam kitchens."

"In the yam kitchens? The queen is in the yam kitchens!"

"Astrahn," the tutor said irritably, "you have been watching over her."

Astrahn was mute for at least a minute, and then he said, "You mean, you mean, that little moppet? The ragamuffin? The forest girl?"

"Yes."

"Who works on the sorting apron, whom we took to the dinner?"

"Yes! Yes!"

"She's the queen. The little girl?"

"She's your queen, general."

Overcome with emotion, Astrahn pulled himself out of his astonishment and said, quietly and resolutely, "The queen lives. All these years, when they thought it was just a dream, it was true. God save the queen."

He was ready to fight now as never before, and he asked for his orders.

"It's now seventeen after two. Can you hold the tower until five past three?"

"If the tower is stormed, we'll do our best."

"You must. Five after three. Hold 'til then, and the kingdom is saved.

Later, Astrahn told me that when he left the regent he saw in his eyes the reflection of the kingdom, marvelously clear, with the sky above and the clouds scudding by like ships.

In the square below, many thousands of scholars had assembled.

Because their rivalries prevented them from associating with one another, they were spread out with remarkable evenness. And as they were naturally timid and not a single one was ignorant of the cavalry sweeps, they tended to stay near the exits. This placement, which he had foreseen, suited the tutor's purposes exactly.

A relatively late arrival at the eastern end of the square was the astronomer Jopincus, a flatterer of the Duke of Tookisheim, whom the Duke of Tookisheim flattered in turn. Hundreds upon hundreds of articles in the *Tookisheim Post* had been devoted to the brilliant Jopincus and his "obviously correct" theory that, if the people did not do exactly what the usurper and the Duke of Tookisheim told them to do, the sun would explode.

And more thousands of articles in the *Tookisheim Post*, on subjects as varied as the self-esteem of female merry-go-round attendants, or the most prestigious way to glaze a mushroom, would begin nonetheless with the words, "Experts agree," or, "It is beyond question," or, "No mainstream scientist would question," followed by "that if everyone does not heed the instructions of the emperor and the Duke of Tookisheim, the sun will explode."

The phrases, "All I know is what the Duke of Tookisheim tells me," and, "All I know is what Peanut Tookisheim tells me," had soon been joined by another: "Do what the emperor says, or the sun will explode."

Jopincus hung back at the eastern end of the square, wondering why the scholars had been turned out when there was no imperial holiday. And he kept checking the clock in the tower, for he knew he would have to leave soon were he to return to his observatory in time to record the full eclipse of the sun at five after three.

Then he caught a glimpse of the tutor, high in the tower, and he put the disparate elements together. As quickly as he could, he ran to find the usurper.

Of course, no one ever knew the usurper's whereabouts, and had Jopincus gone all the way to the headquarters of the Imperial Guard as he had set out to do, he would not have arrived until it was too late. But as he was crossing the Avenue of the Ravens he saw a column of two thousand imperial troops riding toward him, and at their center was the usurper in his chariot.

They would have killed Jopincus merely for blocking their way, had he not been known throughout the kingdom and had he not screamed again and again, "Tell the emperor that I am the astronomer Jopincus and I have an urgent message for him!"

The usurper was, if anything, quick to see a plot, and within a few minutes of receiving Jopincus he wheeled his column about and thundered back down the Avenue of the Ravens toward the tower.

His soldiers ferociously besieged the stairs, and for fifteen minutes Astrahn and his men fought the most difficult battle of their lives. They could not hold the door, which had been immediately blasted open with gunpowder. And though each of their arrows found the heart of one of the Imperial Guard, their stock was soon exhausted and they were able to fire only those shafts that they could retrieve from the cluttered and blood-stained ground on which they fought. In retrieving, they were unduly exposed, and they fell, one by one, until all were killed except Astrahn and Notorincus, who, as the clock struck three, were ten flights from the top with not a single arrow and only Astrahn's sword left with which to fight.

Then a shot rang out, and Astrahn fell. He turned to Notorincus: "Get to the top of the stairs. Protect the regent."

"I have no weapons," Notorincus said, in absolute terror. "What shall I do?"

"Divert them. It's only a matter of minutes. Go!"

Notorincus began the fast climb up ten flights of stairs, with arrows

and crossbow bolts clanging in the railings and against the treads all around him. "I'll never bake another waffle-torte for a single imperial soldier as long as I live!" he said, which was his cry of battle.

Just before the top of the stairs he looked down and saw the soldiers chaining Astrahn before leading him away. Others were flying up the stairs.

Notorincus slammed the clock room door behind him. It had only a small latch, which he set. But as he set it he saw in his mind's eye the metal exploding apart as the door was forced. He hit the door with the heel of his hand and shouted, "No eclairs, you idiots!"

Then he turned toward the balcony landing. The tutor was looking down at him. He had a can of paraffin in one hand and a flaming torch in the other. "Are you all that's left?" the tutor asked.

"Yes, sir," Notorincus answered.

"You're not a soldier."

"No, sir. I'm a baker."

"Can you hold them for two minutes? You don't even have a weapon."

"No, sir, I don't, but I can try to hold them." He turned and looked fearfully toward the sound of boots on the stairs.

"And how do you propose to do that?"

"Ah, well, uh, oh boy, uh, oh," Notorincus said as the first chain-mailed shoulders began to slam against the door. He moved away, toward a looped chain that was rising far into the clock mechanism high above. This was a lift for mechanics, who could exit at many different levels merely by stepping off the rising chain onto little aerial platforms. Thence they could take winding tunnels amid the gears and shafts of light, the cylinders, and the wheels, that ran the clock.

"I'll distract them," Notorincus said, slowly rising, "by taunting them."

The tutor seemed skeptical.

With an explosive burst of sound the door flew open and metal jangled to the floor. Half a dozen soldiers flooded in, stopped, and looked about. They didn't see Notorincus, but they did see the tutor soaking the angel with paraffin. "That's the one!" a soldier said, but as they began to lurch in the direction of the balcony stairs, Notorincus cleared his throat.

"Ahagghham!" he said. "I am the regent of the realm, and here I am, rising up to a rather secret place where I will be able to work a machine that will give your emperor fits."

"You're just a fat slave."

"No. I'm the regent. You don't know that I'm the regent because you're too stupid to walk frontward. Tell me, have you taken your stupid pills today, or did your mother swallow the whole bottle?"

The soldiers were livid. They cranked their crossbows. "Oh," said Notorincus. "Let's see. You think you can hit me at this distance? Most soldiers could put a bolt through the lattice of an apple pullover, but you couldn't hit a spread-eagled hippopotamus."

By now the sun had begun to dim. The tutor was ready to carry the angel to the balcony rail, but he was watching Notorincus slowly rise, and he saw the soldiers lift their crossbows. "I'm the regent!" he shouted. "Not he. Come for me."

"Shut up, old man! We have half a dozen bolts to put in the heart of a slave."

Notorincus cringed. He had nowhere to go. He closed his eyes, and smiled.

The tutor lit the angel and it blazed up bright with silver-gold flame. He bent to its feet and tumbled it over the rail — not of the balcony, as he had planned, but onto the soldiers. They screamed as it fell, and were consumed.

Amid the steady clanking of the machinery, almost at its heart,

Notorincus opened his eyes. As he saw what had happened, those eyes filled with tears, for he knew that the regent of the realm had made the decision to give his life for that of a slave.

"Sir!" he called out as he saw the tutor bathing himself in the remaining paraffin. "Sir! Let *me*! Let *me*!" But eclipses do not last long, and the tutor, besides, was a man of honor who would never have allowed anyone to take his place.

"Tell the queen," the tutor said, "that I love her not because she is our queen, but because she is my daughter. Tell her that when she crosses to the other side of the Veil of Snows, I will be there to take her in my arms."

And then Notorincus watched the regent of the realm step to the rail, torch in hand, and he cried.

By the time the first detachment of soldiers reached the balcony, the tutor was already standing on the rail. They were too late. In a slow and graceful arc he bent the torch to touch his paraffin-soaked garments, and fell forward. As he hurtled through the air the wind made the flames flash. Upon seeing his flight through the dim light of the eclipse the scholars knew that the prophecy was real. They fled the square more quickly than the usurper's soldiers could seal it, and from them the word spread like fire.

They said that as he fell he flew, tumbling and wheeling in the air in slow motion, his arms outspread with all his strength, the fire trailing like the tail of a comet. When the people heard, they knew I had returned and that the kingdom was theirs. And the story of the falling angel would not leave them, for they all had known how my father and mother had died. They were forever moved by this, and, needless to say, so was I.

As word spread, as the armies mobilized, and as a series of blizzards crossed the lake, I was unaware. Laboring day after day in the yam kitchens, I was lost in the darkness and the cold. Had the government decided to send the kingdom's ten-year-old girls to selection I might easily have been caught in the sweeps, but the usurper believed that I had taken refuge in Dolomitia-Swift and would march upon the kingdom with armies raised abroad. He had no idea that within the city he had so carefully sealed, the armies that would defeat him were preparing to rise, or that I was hard at work in one of his forgotten kitchens. I am certain it never would have crossed his mind that the young queen he so feared bathed in yam water and (after I had left my room in the tower) slept on a wooden shelf in a room with forty girls who could neither read nor write.

We awoke in the hours before dawn, and although we could not see the stars, the wagon unloaders told us that early in the morning, when the fewest eyes were open, the stars were at their brightest and most beautiful.

We had only one kerosene lamp. Each day as we struggled to arise, our hands cracked with dryness, our clothes filthy, I would pull on my torn dress in the light of this lamp. Its fumes filled the room, and the ceiling was checkered with soot. The globe and chimney were long blackened, the wick ragged, and the flame broken, but every morning I came to the lamp, and though I shivered and I was sick and I thought there would be no end to my captivity, I saw that the flame, floating upon a level and invisible crystal of vaporized fuel, was pure. I could never find fault with it, or an imperfection in its color, even when all was weakening and all was lost and the world seemed forever dark.

The days and nights fused together in exhaustion. A weak hope would sometimes glint in a vast field of darkness, only to falter and disappear without a sound. Then, as I was working on the apron one

morning, sometimes remembering the mountains, sometimes think-ing not a single thought, the yams stopped rolling down, the lights flickered, and the machinery failed. Never before had this happened. For the first time, we could hear the sounds of boiling and frying be-neath the boiling and frying chutes, and the muffled roars of the yam-eating whatever-they-were far below, and we looked at each other — that is, all the yam curling girls on the apron — and laughed.

Expecting the machinery to start up again, we waited patiently, leaning on our brooms. Nothing happened, so we sat down on the apron and rested. Having absorbed heat from the many fires below it, the iron floor was warm.

"What do you think it is?" one girl asked. I had never heard her speak.

"Perhaps one of the blizzards of February shut down the power-maker," another girl speculated.

"That can't be," said someone else. "The lights are on." And then she said, "You know, if ever I am not a yam curler, I will never look at another yam again. I *hate* yams!"

We laughed, and a freckled red-haired girl said, "You may never look at one, but you'll have them in your dreams for the rest of your life."

Then we heard someone shouting from the far side of the apron:

"Elena's coming! Elena's coming!"

We stood holding our brooms, feigning worry that we had no yams to curl.

"Elena, there are no yams," someone said when she arrived.

"It doesn't matter," Elena answered. "It doesn't matter. Come here, girls. Come to me."

We walked to the edge of the apron. Some of us jumped down. Others remained, holding on to the iron beams that crisscrossed

above. We knew that something had happened, and that things had changed. I breathed lightly, waiting for her to speak, for I sensed that this might be the moment I had been waiting for all my life, even when I had not known it.

Elena looked into the faces and eyes of all the girls who had been on the apron since they were children. They knew nothing else, and this was clear from their expression. But their eyes also showed that they would sense, perhaps better than most, the rising of the wind.

"You think," she said, "that you will be here forever, don't you."

"Will we not?"

"No," she said. "Oh no. You must not think that. You must not despair."

"And why is that?" an older girl asked bitterly.

"You must not despair," Elena said, "for today we have been told a great thing. We have been told that it is true that the child was saved. Long ago, we thought our queen had died." Elena could hardly finish her sentence, and I myself was trembling as she continued. "But a great thing has happened, and this we know for sure. We are not abandoned. The queen has come back. She is among us. She lives."

I knew that this was the beginning, but I did not feel joy, for there was a man that I missed, and I miss him still today. Nonetheless, I had a job to do, and I knew I would be carried through on a long wave of the honor and courage of those who had come before me.

It happened exactly as the tutor had foreseen. After what seemed like an eternity, I finally stood at a closed door beyond which lay the open world and the palace square filled with a million of my soldiers, many of whom would soon give their lives in the fight against the usurper's massive armies.

Before I opened this door, on the other side of which were blue sky and the cold air of winter, I hesitated, for I knew that the simple act of opening it would unleash years of war. I knew that stepping forward meant that whole families would perish, never to be remembered, and that half the kingdom would burn.

But what we had was the same or worse: the deathly clouds of black smoke had never stopped billowing from the distant chimneys. So I prayed for guidance and called upon the memory of my murdered forebears, and when I did I felt their blood in my blood, their hearts in my heart. I pushed at the door. It opened. And all at once the blue sky came flooding in, and the millions in the square fell silent.

BOOK THREE
THE VEIL OF SNOWS

n my room, on a shelf, is a blue bottle of glass so dense and uncorrupted that to look at it or through it is to enter a sapphire, there to be held without breath or desire as if in a world stopped still. It is filled to the top with water from the stream that runs through the village. If you turn it upside down, no bubbles rise. If you peer through the cobalt blue glass you see no indication that the bottle holds a liquid. In fact, did I not know what was in it and were it not so heavy, I would assume that it was empty.

I have had the blue bottle for twenty-five years. The water in the mountains is the best in the kingdom, as prized in the far-off cities even now, in a time of corruption, as it was in a time of purity.

Though I treasure this bottle, the day will come when I drink from it and toss it from my wooden balcony, grateful as it shatters on the rocks below, for on that day all the water that runs through the kingdom will be pure and full of promise, and as life resumes with all its possibilities I will have no need for relics. But until the waiting is done I'll bide my time, as I have been biding it up to now.

I'm hardly content, but I have no choice other than to wait. I chose this place because of the high view it has of the march-lands and the Veil of Snows. Every day I see in the distance sunlit cornices and banks of ice, and bright mists that race across fields of light in pursuit of blinding sunshine. In the saddlebags of the horse I led down from the mountain, I found the bottle that has become the one remaining

object of the old kingdom, the symbol of my hopes and the vanishing point for my devotion.

Many a day has passed when I have forgotten what I am waiting for, and failed to watch the confusing play of light and shadow in the Veil of Snows. Sometimes, I may forget for more than a day. Has it been as long as a week? I think so. Or perhaps several weeks, or a month. Time passes here in its own way, but whether very slow or very fast, it takes you in upon its worlds upon worlds.

And there you always find something, a bright contrast, a surprise that wakes you up, that gives strength and renews faith, even if only because it reminds you of what you've lost and how much you still love. It happened again this morning, when I went to fill a bucket with the water that, charged with the life of the kingdom, will some-day overflow with the vitality of the present. The stream was running so full that I had to go to a different place to draw the water, down the street of stone walls to a windblown pool. Just below this is a weir that foams the stream until it's white with its own velocity and strength.

I'm not young. I was tired from carrying the empty bucket, and dreaded carrying it back full, especially up the stairs, so I sat upon a bench that with the rising of the stream was now so close to the rapid that I felt as if I were riding on the back of a swan swirling on the tide. I breathed the fresh air that rose from the agitated current and let my head fall back until my eyes were filled with perfectly blue sky resting upon the pointed rooftops of gabled wooden houses. As I stared past the fronts of yellowing varnish and boxes of blood-red geraniums I was thinking neither of the queen I loved, nor of the Veil of Snows, nor of her son who vanished there. I was merely old and tired, and passing time in the sun. I don't remember how long this lasted, but

after the shadows rose and fell and I felt rested, I picked up the bucket and knelt by the edge of the river. I dipped the bucket in and pulled out what seemed to be just air and sun as white as snow, and as the white water settled into the clear, I watched half of what I had drawn out simply disappear.

As I was thinking about this I looked down at the stream, and there running swiftly past me on top of the foam were clotted chains of scarlet and crimson, tangling, sinking, diluting, and disappearing. My bucket fell into the torrent, never to be seen again, and I staggered back, electrified by memories of a different time.

The crimson and scarlet lines were not the blood of men, women, and horses, but merely dye that a laundress had loosed for an instant upon the stream. As fast as it had appeared, it was gone, perhaps chasing the lost bucket, and the water was white so soon afterward that I wondered if I had imagined this, especially when I looked up to see that the laundress I had glimpsed was no longer there.

Having come to fetch water, there I was without a bucket, next to a river speeding by in immense volumes of foam and spray carried upon cold black currents in obsidian gleams. And there I was, an old man in the sun, about to begin the difficult walk home, up thirsty hills and thirsty steps, to a house in which the only water that awaited me was in the blue bottle.

Though once I was a singer of tales, they were not very good, for I always put too much of my heart in them, and never enough (I was told) of calculation. Where others would captivate and entertain, I would only sing a simple song that bent its head as if in prayer before time and truth and love. It was all I could do, and all I

wanted to do, and I don't know why. I followed nature's wild rivers and God's glittering lights, and they led me into a land where I was alone.

I was neither afraid of my solitude nor unhappy about it, but, lacking an audience, I could no longer be a singer of tales, and I became what I am now, which is I don't exactly know what. Perhaps I am a kind of sentinel. My little house is high on a hillside overlooking the village, and from only mediocre height it has a commanding view of the great march-lands and the Veil of Snows. But though a sentinel, I do not merely watch. I wait, and I have formed an image of exactly what it is I hope to see.

Long ago, in the time of the old emperor, I was young and just beginning in my profession. The usurper was there, and one could not escape his evil presence. With his inexhaustible schemes, numerous agents, and terrific powers he often seemed about to prevail, but the old emperor, who had been through many more battles than he, always held him in check. That there was a struggle between what was, in the main, good, and what was, in the main, evil, and that time after time the good prevailed, made all the children born in my time believe that this was the natural order of things, that even if it took a great deal of effort, effort would always find its reward and the just would triumph, as would the innocent.

I still believe, which is why I am on a hillside waiting. And I certainly believed then, even as the usurper began to gain the upper hand. Surely, I thought, the crimes that bring him power will soon bring him down. Waiting then, as now, I did not change my songs, as did the other singers who listened carefully to everything that was new, and soon I found that I was nowhere, they were everywhere, and the usurper had taken the throne.

Can you imagine my surprise the day that he sent for me? Why would he bother with a singer of the old songs? Why would he bother with me? But he did bother. He cared inordinately, as if his life depended on it, as if I were his most vexing opponent. This I could hardly believe, and not only was I flattered, I was so afraid that my heels shook as if in an earthquake. As soon as he began to speak, however, I realized that I need not have feared. Either he would kill me, and I would have eternal peace, or I would beat him with courage alone. Were he not actually three times my size, he certainly appeared to be, and this was multiplied by his rank and disdain.

"You are still singing tales in the old style?" he asked, his voice as sharp as the point of a lance and as deep as the beat of a drum.

"Yes."

"Where?"

"Well," I said, "times have been rather tough. I sang by a merchant's campfire not so long ago. A caravan was taking empty lard cans to the nether outskirts of Zilna."

"How many?"

"How many lard cans?"

"No, idiot! How many merchants?"

"One. "

"You said a merchants' campfire."

"Yes, a merchant, and his campfire."

"You sang to one person? Isn't that demeaning?"

"I've had worse."

"You've had audiences of less than one?"

"My career has had its ups and downs. It is possible to sing to no one, and lately I've been doing that quite a lot."

As if remembering his own difficult times, the usurper nodded. For my part I prayed that I would not begin to like him, although I cared very little if he liked me or not, for I knew that even were he extremely fond of me he could have me dispatched as easily as cracking a pumpkin seed. He had passions, and he sometimes killed for them, but he killed most often and most vigorously out of calculation, for to him all of life was a battle, and the object of the battle was to conquer all.

"Why is it then, that my agents call you a threat?"

I suppose he wanted me to write my own dismissive obituary before he killed me, but, in defiance, I would not. "They tell you, Emperor, that I am a threat, because I am a threat."

"Singing to a single merchant about to journey a thousand miles with a bunch of empty lard cans?"

"Even had I sung just to the cans themselves."

"And how is that?"

"As long as I sing, a song is there. And if a song is there, someone might hear it and sing it to someone else, who would in turn sing it to someone else, and so on and so forth, until eventually it might become the anthem of the armies that will send you to oblivion."

"Then I shall have you killed."

"I was not expecting otherwise, and it hardly matters. My songs, though not very popular, will remain. The Damavand sing them even now. And someday their horsemen, riding at the head of the armies, will have cause to sing indeed. You are using actualities to fight potentialities, and that, Emperor, is a worse nightmare than any you can visit upon me."

"We'll see," he said, in a voice so deep that the chalices shook.

I was expecting to die right then and there, but he said, "I order you to unravel your singing."

"I beg your pardon?"

"Unravel it!"

"Meaning, sir?"

"Your songs," he said, impatiently. "Un*do* them."

"I can't. They're already sung."

"Then sing them again, differently. Sing them so that they are about me. Sing them so that when people hear them they will weep for my sacrifices and admire my powers."

At this I laughed, which must have astonished him, knowing as he did what he had in mind for me. "I would not laugh if I were you," he warned.

"Why not laugh?" I asked. "I know how you will torture me, but I know that I will not sing the songs as you would have me sing them. You might as well try to burn water, because I'm water, and water doesn't burn."

I then spent the next years of my life — the longest years I remember—in the deepest torture chambers underneath the loftiest prisons. By some chance or interference I refused to die, day after day, until finally the armies of the young queen captured the city and freed us all. No longer a singer, and fit only to be a soldier, I joined the victorious armies just as most everyone else was leaving them. Of low rank, broken memories, and no prospects, I knew nonetheless that a new struggle was inevitable.

It was a summer victory, I was freed in August, and I passed into the ranks on a cold and rainy day in September, the first day of a season that can be either bleak or clear. The induction hall was cheerful as soldiers mustered out, moving into the newly liberated civilian world. The place itself had been an army watch station, of which the old emperor had built a hundred, and the usurper a further nine hundred. They were all of stone and heavy timber, with vast spaces, and fireplaces so gargantuan that in one of them half a dozen cooks were working amid just as many tables and three or four separate blazes, all under a single mantel.

"This is one of the usurper's former watch stations," said the sergeant in charge, really a baker I had run into from time to time before the revolt. He was a strange man, small and fat, as furry as a baby bear, with two enormous and blazingly white front teeth. His name was Notorincus, and though his bearing was entirely unmilitary, he was a capable soldier.

"How do you know it wasn't built by the old emperor?" I asked.

"The torture chambers underneath."

"Ah yes. The torture chambers," I replied, with no evident emotion.

"And also, these barracks, which have not been enlarged, hold a hundred men. The old emperor's watch stations held fifty. All he needed throughout the city were five thousand soldiers, and they had nothing to do. With a hundred men at a thousand stations, the usurper had a hundred thousand, and they never rested."

Notorincus saw that I glanced repeatedly at the cooks. "Are you hungry?" he asked.

"I'm very hungry."

"That's no reason to join the army."

"Of course. My hunger and my enlistment are coincidental."

"Still," he said, almost brushing me away, as bureaucrats do when they imagine that in signaling a person out of the room by making sweeping motions over their desk they are doing God's will, "why don't you eat and then come back, to see if you really want to join. I'll account it as a recruitment expense."

I agreed. The cooks at the nearest fireplace were stirring something in a huge cauldron. "What's in here?" I asked, and the answer was provided by a woman in Balarian cap and gown.

"First," she said, "we roast venison, wild turkey, boar, and pheasant, continually drenching them in a marinade of red wine and fresh herbs. Then we slice the meat and throw it into the cauldron. We add pure water carted here from the mountains, and as this cooks we prepare the vegetables. We roast potatoes, parboil carrots and celery, and braise half a dozen wild lettuces, armandellos, and spoots that have flavors both strong and subtle.

"All is added together to boil and simmer for many hours. It is a royal recipe that the queen has made the army's own. You may have some, but don't eat too much. You cannot be fat in the army." She looked at Notorincus, seemed embarrassed, looked at me who was still starved, and cast her eyes down.

As I am not the kind of person who would join the army for a meal, I returned to Notorincus after I had eaten, and he took down my history and questioned me about my fall. "Why didn't you simply alter your songs?" he asked, gazing at my scars, of which there are so many that even to this day I can be only a man alone.

"I couldn't."

"Why?"

"They had already been sung. They existed."

"But why not change them as requested?"

This question puzzled me. "Never was there the possibility that I would do that."

"Why?" Notorincus pressed.

"I suppose it's because they're like people," I said. "They may be like dumb or ugly people, or people who are deformed, but I couldn't just take their names, annihilate them, and issue new ones, could I?"

"I suppose not, if you think they're like people, but are they really?"

"Yes," I answered, nodding. "They have in them something, sometimes a great deal, of the people I love, some of whom are lost forever. Therefore, I could not have split them like wood, or carved them like stone. It would have been a betrayal, and it would have corrupted the world."

"The whole world?"

"Just my part of it," I said, "but that is, after all, the part for which I am responsible."

"You would have died rather than abandon the old songs?"

"Yes."

"But life is so precious."

"Yes."

"It is paramount."

"No."

"No? Then what is?"

"Love," I said, "and honor."

"Excellent!" said Notorincus. "Excellent! I'm sending you directly to the Queen's Own Guard, my regiment. You don't look very good, but we'll get you back on your feet and train you until you are master of horse, sword, and bow. I myself came to the ranks knowing virtually nothing, and now I'm nothing but a soldier.

"You were a baker, weren't you?"

"You knew me?"

"I remember your stand at the night skating."

"I can still bake, I haven't forgotten. It's like riding a bicycle. Sometimes a brioche or a Sacher torte appears in our barracks," he said, "quite mysteriously."

"I see."

"And you? Can you still sing tales? The queen loves the singing of tales."

"No," I answered. "I cannot. I have in me only one more tale, and I must wait to see it before I can sing it."

Soon after I had been trained, I was brought to the queen. Service first as a conscript in the old emperor's army and then as a reservist had made horse, sword, and bow part of my nature, but I did require a year to regain my health and strength. A little more than a year, actually, and Notorincus escorted me to the royal apartments in October, when the mountains were gold and the air was bright.

Though the queen could have had a hundred fires burning and never had to tend a one, she kept a small blaze in a modest terra cotta stove the size of an orange crate, and this she took care of herself, with evident pleasure, feeding in new wood and stirring the coals with a plain wrought-iron poker. I don't imagine that the usurper has ever touched such a thing, as even the handles of his heaviest swords and most horrible maces are filled in white gold.

I was surprised by the modesty of the royal quarters. Though some of her tables were of spectacular intarsia and the oldest, darkest, most glowing woods in the world, others were of pine and quite rough. A huge painting of the battle of Valò made one wall a world of color, but on another a long peg rack held swords and bows, quivers of arrows, coils of rope, military clothes, and leather saddlebags filled with bedding, food, and tools. The queen, who had since childhood been a soldier and who took nothing for granted, including her station, was to be proved horribly right.

But at that time the victory had just been won, adversaries

pardoned, prisoners released, soldiers returned, and she could freely show all the beauty of her youth and triumph. I confined my emotions to loyalty. As one of the queen's common subjects, a soldier in her guard, and a much older man, I was not free to fall in love with her, so I did not. She had taken a husband in any case, I was of no rank, and, after my time in the cells, women looked away from me.

The queen did not, and her loveliness of soul, directness, her grace, and her high qualities washed over me with such delightfulness, shock, and strength that I was awakened and renewed. She was only eighteen or twenty, and her long hair, which in her youth had been golden, had in its dark chestnut color no hint whatsoever of brittleness or fatigue. Her face had no sign of flagging energy, self-indulgence, or defeat, as do the faces, if you look closely, of even many twenty-year-olds.

Hers was the kind of beauty that does not proclaim, but listens. Hers was the beauty of gentleness and trust, of devotion. She was dressed in gray, with a scarlet and gold medallion below her left shoulder, and, wonder of wonders for a royal, who is not expected to show any kind of weakness, she wore spectacles. Thin tortoise shell, the same rich brown color as her hair, they held lenses of such clear crystal that the transparency generated touches of gleaming silver.

This was our queen, whom I loved the moment I looked upon her, for whom I would sacrifice, for whom I would die, and whom I would obey. Once I had seen her from a distance, upon a balcony, and that was enough to make me twice loyal. But in her presence my life changed, as did my purpose, which is what royalty are for, though mostly they strive and fail to imitate those few, like the queen, who give to the word *royal* its meaning and good name.

I sank to one knee and bowed as I was required both by cus-

tom and my own heart, and, by God, all in surprise, she took a
sword and knighted me. I, a broken man, a good soldier, a failed
singer — a knight!

"Rise!" she commanded. And, as I stood, I looked into her face.

"Madam," I said, my voice choked with emotion. "I don't understand."

"Do not feel that you have been chosen without merit or in damag-
ing haste. I took command of the armies as a child, a girl. I was not a
man, and could not make my decisions as a man. I was not old, and
could not make them from experience. And because the fate of all
rested upon them, I learned to draw from depths that others were not
forced to find. I learned to act with the speed of a hawk tucking in its
wing for a dive. Perhaps I might have been more deliberate, but the
opportunity was not there, and I for the rest of my life must do things
the way salmon jump, waves roll, and trees bend."

Notorincus, who had remained, smiled, because he had been with
her in victory after victory, and when she had risen from defeat.

"At the battle of Lichtengaard, over which I presided when still a
child — it was the first major battle of my life — one of the soldiers
in the ranks was singing a song of yours, only one soldier, and I took
from it a line that I have carried in my heart ever since, for not only
did it serve me that day, but when I say it even now I feel love and
truth as if they are waves that are lifting me from the ground."

I did not ask what line it was, and she did not tell in this, my first
meeting with her, and though I was in her guard and frequently saw
her from afar, some years would pass before the next.

Again she called for me in the fall, but this time in November, when gray skies rolled with dark woolly clouds, and the fire in the terra cotta stove was bigger and brighter. She seemed much more a woman now, though not too much time had passed, and of course I went down on one knee and all that, but though I was thrilled to see her I didn't smile or glow the way people do in the presence of royalty. I wasn't there to have my buttons polished but to serve queen and country. And this she knew, which is why she called for me.

"The father of my child," she said, holding her baby up in the air and moving him to and fro until he smiled with the game, "has seen him only once. All this time, he has been at the head of the armies, in the march-lands, with the Damavand. My husband is used to living in the open, used to moving under the weight of armor and sword, used to cutting the flow of streams with the passage of his war horses, used to directing men with nothing in their eyes but the cold blue sky. And yet, when he came to his son, he held him with tenderness such as I have never seen, he rocked him, and kissed him, and tears fell from his eyes onto his polished armor.

"Soldiers fear that their children will be left without them in a cruel and pitiless world, that they will not be able to pass on to them the skills of self-preservation. My husband said, 'The boy and I must ride together so that I may teach him to be the match of any enemy. Already I am plotting to make him a master of horse, this infant, this tiny baby, whom I must leave so soon, though I hope not forever.' That is what he said, and then he had to leave.

"As queen, it is my duty to ensure that mothers may teach daughters, and fathers may ride with their sons, for from the beginning of time these have been among the best of things that some seek to overthrow."

"Who?" I asked.

"Who? Those who cannot abide by simple beauties and things of the heart. Those who chafe at unreformed tranquility. Those who would tear parent from child for the sake of ambition or idea." She went to the window, and I followed. When she walked she moved as smoothly as a swan gliding through water.

"Look over the streets," she commanded, and I did, easily, for although her apartments were modest they had a stunning view. The city was spread below us as if we were standing on a cloud. "There you can see a hunting party coming in after a day in the fields. Soaked by squalls and buffeted by the wind, their oilskins are glistening, their eyes bright, cheeks red, and noses cold. Their bags are filled with stiff and bloody birds, their limbs are sore, and their hearts contented. Tonight they will eat and drink, and then sleep deep sleep by the fire, with dreams of primal things, of arrows flying, blue skies scalloped with black cloud, of death and the rain.

"And yet these are only hunters. They pass through unguarded gates and troop through the city in peace, but when I hear the hoof-beats of their horses I think of battle. In quiet times I think of nothing but that."

"You were raised in battle."

"Yes. I've done my best to learn the peace, but cannot."

"As long as the sword is sheathed until it is needed, you have committed no sin."

"Ah," she said, no longer reflective, but with fervor, "that's not what the Duke of Tookisheim says! Oh no! He, his mouthpieces, newspapers, broadsheets, and criers, say quite the opposite. They say that to be prepared is a danger to the peace, and that the implements and skills of war must be abolished."

"And what of the usurper? What if he is spit from the Veil of Snows, an army behind him and a week's march from our gates?"

"As the *Tookisheim Post* said only yesterday," the queen said, placing her spectacles upon the bridge of her nose, and then letting them slide down a bit before she read, " 'such an event is highly unlikely, hardly imaginable, next to impossible. The last time a pretender returned from the Veil of Snows was in the time of the old emperor's tenth grandfather. Indeed, the last time anyone is reliably reported to have come from the mists was a full year ago, when a man dressed as a shepherd suddenly appeared on the snowfield above Mannisbreim, utterly confused and from no one knows where. Why is it, then, that our resources are wasted in keeping the prince and his substantial armies at the margins of the kingdom, guarding against nothing more than a figment of the queen's disturbed imagination?' " She slowly removed her spectacles, and looked up at me in gorgeous agitation.

"In the ranks, Majesty," I said, "soldiers ask why you have not exiled, executed, or imprisoned the Tookisheims, although they know the answer, and are just expressing hope."

"Of course they know. I cannot exile, execute, or imprison a man solely on account of his opinion, which is what the usurper did. We are confident that in the wars of opinion, our views will prevail, and, if not, then not."

"Even if the fields are tilted? Nay, vertical?"

The queen cocked her head in anger. "I do not understand why every newspaper in the land, every broadsheet and every crier, is owned by the Duke of Tookisheim, or Peanut the idiot son, or, now, after the return migrations of the usurper's Damavand colonists, by other dreadful, vulgar, cheap, and grasping Tookisheims.

"I lose count. Let me see. Branco Tookisheim, from Bulgatia, makes the talking boxes that take the place of books. My statisticians tell me that he is now the richest man in the kingdom, richer even than his uncle, and much admired as a seer, although he sees nothing. How could he see anything in those diminutive little boxes full of stupid shifting colors that, when all is said and done, add up to nought?

"Bulgis Tookisheim, Branco's always unctuous brother, has corrupted the schools of the kingdom beyond imagining. I have no authority in this question, never having attended school, but in my visits I have seen that the classes are devoted to absolutely everything but study. All is games, costumes, tricks, machines, travel, politics, superstition, and entertainment."

"I know, Majesty. I was graduated from these schools before Bulgis Tookisheim made them into madhouses and penny arcades. I grieve for the students, who are obliged to float through hurricanes of idiocy."

The queen raised her left arm to a level just above her shoulder, opened her hand, let it drop, and said, with animation and despair, "The kingdom is judged anew with each generation. If its children are corrupted and distracted, the kingdom will fall. I believed after the victory that our satisfaction and relaxation would be of short duration, that memory would serve to keep us on an even keel, that having been through suffering and danger we would from the day of our freedom be responsible and true. But no. The same parties that want to disband the armies also want to punish the vanquished, who will rise against us so much the faster if they know we are weak. What is it in these people that makes them turn the wheel to which they are pinned until their heads hang once again under their heels?

"We, who should be temperate, magnanimous, hard-working, strong, well armed, and kind, are instead flighty, vindictive, lazy, weak, disarmed, and cruel. The cities are full of the casualties of love

225

overthrown, children abandoned, and vows broken. Our diminished armies exist in the splendor of the open air, disciplined and true, but at home they are denounced. If this kingdom were not my own, I would look upon it with disdain, distrust it in alliance, and believe others in their grievances against it. I know well what will come of this. As in the blink of an eye, comfort will become peril. Suddenly, all of us — the weak, the vain, the honest, and the iron-willed—shall know nothing but war and death. How can I prevent this? I am the queen. I have powers, and it is my duty to set things right. You, who know a thousand tales, draw from them, reach back, and say what I might do."

We stood in silence, looking over the city as squalls of rain and fronts of cloud swept from district to district, now lightening, now darkening, but always moving. The lake was ruffled in blue and gray, whitecaps visible as a gloss half gone the moment it was perceived. Evening was approaching, and lines of smoke rose from countless fires that gave the air the scent of cedar and pine. I said nothing, for what I might have said would have been far worse than staying silent, and when the queen saw this, her heart seemed to break, for she was the queen, and it was her duty to see into the vales of sorrow.

As things had worsened from month to month and year to year, celebrations and distractions had become more common. When the kingdom had been moving forward with all good speed and great things were done every day, no one celebrated, for the celebration was in the doing, and our hearts were full. But when nothing seemed to work, and even the river seemed to flow only in fits and starts, the air was never clear, and the streets were never clean, the world exploded in dinner parties, ceremonies, awards, commemorations, banquets, feasts, contests, meetings, all the meaningless gleanings that were the realm of the perpetually busy Tookisheims.

The Tookisheims. The Duke, Peanut, Branco, Bulgis, Rand from Aramonia, Marco, Firco, Jocko, Bruno, Fippo, and Blottis from the Herring Flats, Malitia and Sucritan Tookisheim who ran the circuses, Rolf who made dresses, Ipwog from so far away that no one knew whence he had come, and Minty and Wissy and Patricia and Minka Tookisheim, females of the clan who had married advantageously and outlived four husbands who all had died coincidentally on the same day, of plum poisoning. And then there was little Walnut Tookisheim, Peanut's brat, who went about in a cart drawn by eight poor children, and Beanslaw Tookisheim, the electricity magnate, who made his fortune by harnessing dynamos to house-size wheels in which ten thousand chipmunks fed on meal laced with anxiety drugs would desperately try to flee overhead horns blasting out *The 1812 Overture*.

They were all over the place — not the chipmunks, whom boys trapped and sold to Beanslaw Tookisheim's agents for a derma apiece (because, needless to say, the chipmunks on the wheel had no time for courtship, marriage, and reproduction), but Tookisheims, that is; Tookisheims, Tookisheims, all around, and not a one could think. It was impossible to turn one's head without catching sight of something that had to do with a Tookisheim. Born with neither reticence nor sorrow, they charged forward from their first day to the last, convincing themselves with the progress of their success that they were worthy and good, when all the time they were hardly human and made the world so miserable that if it had been a dog it would have begged to be put to sleep.

Even the queen could not remain wholly without their orbit, and one night she went into their midst, in the time when the lights had begun to go out all across the kingdom. I was on the ramparts, guarding in bright moonlight as the queen attended a dinner honoring

Peanut Tookisheim's induction into the hall of fame of the Savarins of Tropical Nuts. Peanut, you see, was a moron who, although he ran all the newspapers in the land, could not write an article that anyone could understand. They all went something like this: "Morbopus, when, after which and in which specifically it was that it did not, much less to say if then it would not, then, certainly, that which it did but with which it cannot and absolutely has to have did." His father had to establish the Savarins of Tropical Nuts so that Peanut, who was able to tell one nut from another, could collect some ribbons and sashes, which were de rigueur for any Tookisheim.

The queen had been blackmailed into attending the dinner when the Duke of Tookisheim hinted to her that if she did not he would strop the news until the ragpickers went into rebellion and with senseless and febrile abandon dived off the parapets by the hundreds or thousands.

So she steeled herself and went. As a soldier of the close guard, I stood immediately outside the dining room, on the rampart of one of the Duke of Tookisheim's pieds-à-terre embedded in the wall in one of the fashionable districts on the lake. The moon was shining in bright silver, cascading across the waters in an oxygenless beam, and were it not for the pure imbibition of its cold light I would have been seasickened by the conversation from the banquet, of which I heard every word.

Though they hated her, the Tookisheims were absolutely tickled to be in the presence of the queen, and they gushed, burped, bloated, and moaned like infatuated hippopotamuses, as the poor queen could hardly stay afloat in the torrents, lakes, and sinkholes of Tookisheim vanity and inanity.

One is supposed neither to speak first nor to argue in the presence

of the queen, but before she had even sat down, Rand and Blottis were going hot and heavy — screaming, gesticulating, standing and then being pushed back into their chairs by their footmen — about which was the more challenging game, ring toss or quoits. Were it not for the carefully observed commandment against inter-Tookisheim fratricide they probably would have duelled that night, struggling home after twenty minutes of swordplay with hundreds of pulled muscles and not a single cut.

"Aren't the two games almost exactly alike?" the queen asked, amazed.

"Oh no, Majesty," Rand and Blottis said, as if twinned. "They're much different! That's because, that's because, that's because. . . ." And there they froze, and were to remain frozen, mouths open, eyes staring vacantly ahead, for the rest of the dinner. On account of the splendid acoustics of the vaulted stone ceiling, I heard the queen say quietly to herself, "Two down."

I was just beginning to smell the quick-grilled miniature Dolomitian salmon (which are filleted and marinated after being kept without food for a week in fresh spring water). Half a fish, sans head and tail and flavored with oil and herbs, is thrown for an instant on a white-hot grill, flipped like a live fish rising momentarily from the mirrored surface of a lake, and then charred on the other side. Not only do they sizzle, but the Duke of Tookisheim served them without limit, and to cool the palate he provided an argon sherbet.

"What is that, exactly?" I heard the queen ask.

"A gas, Majesty. My chefs purify it from the air. They run after it with butterfly nets and collect it in platinum flagons. Then it's chilled with a hazelnut-clotted-cream-raspberry puree. A dash of cherry brandy, and . . . *voilà.*"

"I didn't think," said the queen, "that even the imperial kitchens in the time of the usurper, when they were stoked into activity as white hot as the grills for Dolomitian salmon, produced such rarities."

The Tookisheims had strained to the limits of human discipline not to mention the usurper in front of the queen, only to have the queen bring him up herself. They did not know what to say. Although they had feared the usurper as much as they had profited from serving him, they had come to profit more in the freedom of the restoration, and although they generally preferred to his dictatorship their own peculiar form of government, known among scholars as an idiocracy, they wanted him to return nonetheless because they needed his wafer-thin moral pretenses, his baroque lies, his insatiable desire for the foppish, the vacant, the fashionable and cruel — in short, for the essence of Tookisheimness. (Once, Blottis had manufactured a perfume that he called *Mooplah — The Essence of Tookisheim.*)

"Majesty," said Peanut, in a moment of candid idiocy, "we are keeping the usurper's traditions alive."

Though the other Tookisheims froze, the queen did not. "Yes, Peanut," she said. "I know. And half the kingdom, transfixed by Branco's little boxes, shares your hope for his return."

Trying to be diplomatic, the duke broke in. "Majesty, Branco sells ten thousand of his boxes each day."

"And the boxes," Branco added with pride and hysteria, "are nothing! What matters," he continued, holding out his left index finger and twisting it in the air as if he were impaling an invisible Lilliputian, "is the cards that go inside. I sell a box for fifty derma, but the box costs me forty-five derma to produce. I sell a card for fifteen derma, that has cost me one derma to produce. And for every box, I sell a dozen cards a year. Do you know how many derma pour in each hour? I need one of my boxes and a set of cards to calculate it. And what's so wonderful about all this is that I don't even have to do any work. Various idiots make up the cards, other idiots put them in nice packages, and other idiots sell them. It's like a factory. It is a factory. A money factory! I have so many derma I don't even know what to do with them. I can't explain it, but I love being rich, and the richer I get, the richer I want to be!"

"It was like that, I'm told," the queen said plaintively, "in the time of the cloth merchants."

"But that was only cloth, and these are boxes with colors!" Branco shouted.

"That was only cloth," the queen repeated, "that fell from a woman's shoulder and flowed with her as she danced, that swaddled a newborn, that kept the hunter warm as snow choked the air. Just cloth. . . .

"Whereas," she went on, having gotten used to writing decrees all day, "you, Branco, with your ugly little boxes and cards, have taken the stream of life, the wind, the cold, the oxygen, and the air, and made them a game. Branco, I have known sweat and blood, the scent of the woods, the smell of a fire, ice breaking up on a lake, the cold, the dark, the August sun, real kisses, true love, loyalty, suffering, and sacrifice. But Branco, I hate, I hate, I truly hate . . . games. And you, Branco Tookisheim," she said, her lovely eyes burning through him like a hot brand, "are turning the life of my kingdom into knock hockey."

"But Majesty," said Peanut, smiling weakly, "Branco's boxes do all kinds of things. They count the number of peanuts at the peanut exchange. They keep track of the moisture content in millions of hazelnuts. They monitor cashews!"

"How extraordinary," said the queen, so disdainfully that some of the candles were snuffed out. But then the next course was served — medallions of smoked wild turkey with truffled artichoke puree — and in the rich silence each Tookisheim stewed, wondering what disaster would be next, for it was after all a sad thing that this whole race of men, these idiots and fops, could only offend and anger the queen. My heart was heavy, for I knew how unhappy she was that all our triumphs were turning to brittle glass, so resolutely, so fast. That evening, nothing anyone might have said would have charmed her. Her husband, unaccounted for unusually long, weeks past the customary point, was encamped near the Veil of Snows, and though she longed to be with him, the capital and its governance required her presence. Her infant son, whom she held most of the day as she wrote decrees and sat in councils, was alone in his crib while she dined with idiots dressed like Spanish grandees in lace, wigs, and fly's-eyed-green satin that clasped their undisciplined bellies like luxury coverlets knit for pregnant watermelons.

These Tookisheims, I thought, and was just about to fulminate in a sentry's eye-darkening finger-pointing diatribe, when I heard a faint sound from over the wall. Though it hardly registered, it was real enough to choke my resentful monologue, and a good thing too, for never was there an angry song worth the singing. Was the sound that of a bird passing by the battlements, ghostlike against the stars? The sky was empty. Another sentry, trying to signal? I looked to left and right: all was well. Something from inside? No, it had risen on the wind.

I went to the parapet and looked over the dizzying sides of moonlit stone. The sound of waves far below combined with the hiss of air in the teeth of the battlements. Only a thin scallop of rock lay between the base of the wall and the lake, dark and wet from the hooking of whitecaps. The sole way to get there was by boat. I heard the sound

again. It was a cry. And then I saw movement far beneath me. I called the sergeant of the guard, and instructed him to bring ropes, and although it took some time, he did.

I suppose I ruined that dinner by trooping my soldiers through the dining room under huge coils of rope. The Duke of Tookisheim came out, about to burst with screams he could not release because of the presence of the queen, and tried to slash me with his gaze. But his gaze was not very sharp, and what did I care? His newspapers had never published any of my songs in the days when newspapers had things in them other than articles about artichokes, and now my time of singing tales was over and I was a soldier of the queen.

"What are you doing with these twines?" he asked.

"Twines?"

"Yes. Strings."

"Ropes, you mean, or lines?"

"Lines, twines, I don't care, you're dragging them through the dinner of the century! We're celebrating Peanut's induction as a . . . oh, never mind. The queen is here, you can't do this!"

As he twitted, I was grateful to be lowered over the parapet at the end of the rope, where I found myself alone in the moonlight next to the elemental rock of a face so sheer that it was visited only by sun, wind, and snow. How graceful it is in such lonely places, how tranquil to sink slowly into the abyss, awake and alive.

Halfway down, the waves began to sound like a storm, and I could see a figure lying prone on the rock below. As I was nearing the ground I began to feel the cold spray of fresh water from the shrapnel of the waves. My right foot touched the ground in absolute silence, as if I weighed an ounce, and I felt like an angel. The lake, like a sea, was rolling, broken with white, and freezing cold, and immediately before me was a child, a girl of about eight, in homespun cotton encrusted with ice. On the rocks nearby, splintered and broken, were the remains of a crude round boat called a rowell, used by the fishermen in the swamps southeast of the lake, off the narrow bay that stretches for many a day's travel to meet the inrush of the river Darya.

As I removed my coat and wrapped her in it, she hardly moved. Not expecting her to speak, I began to tie a harness into the rope, intending to loop it around her tiny waist and chest so that she could ride up with me, but as I was doing this she jumped back.

Nothing I could say reassured her, and every time I took a step in her direction she herself stepped back, until she was standing dangerously close to the water. Then I fell back a little, and she moved toward me the same distance. With no idea what to do, I sent up a note describing the situation and requesting some food with which, perhaps, to gain her trust.

When the rope came down toward us, I thought it had a huge basket tied to it, and then I thought this was a soldier. How stupid, I thought, to send a man down when a basket or a sack would do. But it was neither a basket, nor a sack, nor a soldier, it was the queen.

I smiled to think how she must have stunned the Tookisheims, doing what they would only pay someone to do, someone whose life they thought damnable and disposable. And so it was with many kinds of satisfaction that I sank to my knees and made a deep bow, as is required when the queen comes into one's presence, even if one has been standing on the rampart all evening listening to her speak.

Whereas I had been tied securely, she had simply stepped into a loop in the rope. I was not surprised. Royal beings make their own safety and have their own style of grace. The minute she alighted she rushed to the child and warmed her with her arms, and the child,

knowing the embrace that protected her was that of the sovereign, did not object. But, still, she would not speak.

"A long time ago," the queen told her, "I arrived in this city in much the same way you have, with perhaps the same fears and the same foreboding, but I learned not to be afraid, I grew, my heart strengthened, and I even became a queen. In the very first days, I trusted myself to a rope that lifted me to a high place where I had never been. Now you must trust me to take you up. It shouldn't be that hard. I was alone then, but you are not."

She put her foot into the loop, bent slightly, and took the child up, thanks to my hard-working infantrymen, as smoothly as two birds on a column of wind slipping past the sun-baked granite of a summer cliff. Soon after, I followed.

The Tookisheims, those idiot Tookisheims, just sat at the table looking on disapprovingly as the child quivered from exhaustion and cold. "She needs a bed until the doctor comes," the queen announced.

"These are business premises," the Duke of Tookisheim said archly. "We have no beds. There is no place here for dirty children from the street." He thought this well said, and a slight smile raised the corners of his mouth, near the artificial birthmarks.

"You're saying that there is no place for this child to lie down, no food for her at a table overladen with food?"

"Majesty," the duke said, his tone offensively instructional, "royalty should avoid proximity to the wretched and lowborn."

"She needs something to eat," the queen said, almost in tears.

The Duke of Tookisheim mistook this for weakness, the first unraveling, perhaps, of her authority. "Not this food," he said, "not here."

Our queen, though judicious and true and always restrained in the use of her great power, was not absolutely perfect. She was, thank

241

God, a creature of passion, who sometimes abandoned all she knew and all she had learned for the sake of a simple thing that spoke directly to her heart.

When she extended her lithe and powerful arm, and swept everything off the table, it was, I suppose, the beginning of the end. Like shot from a cannon, the crystal, the goblets, the silver, the chalices, the stemware, the dishes, the plates, and the salvers rocketed from the linen and smashed against the wall.

How wonderful to see such a beautiful queen so livid and enlivened. "You!" she commanded, in a voice that was irresistibly powerful and yet lovely and feminine at the same time — a perfect alto. "You Tookisheims! For you I now invoke the charter of national defense and declare a state of emergency. Until further notice you are impressed into my military service, with the rank, each and every one of you, of garbage handler."

"I'm a brigadier-general in the reserve!" Bulgis protested.

"You were a brigadier-general, Bulgis, and until you find work in the military garbage brigade you and the other Tookisheims will attend to this child. Her blankets shall be the finest of your damasks, her bed the great table, her food the food you were about to eat."

"Like hell!" shouted Branco, stepping back a pace, his eyes on the queen and flashing in anger. This was the beginning of rebellion, or would have been, for the instant he began to draw his sword against the queen herself, I drew mine. And by the time his sword was ready to straighten after its weak opening arc, I had killed him. Quickly following upon that, our men drew their weapons, and the Tookisheims sank to their knees and bowed, though not out of reverence.

"Arrest them," the queen said. "We'll have to let them go, but arrest them now, bring the child food and bedding, and hurry the doctor."

She turned to me. "Are we back in the days of struggle?" she asked. "Is this how it begins?"

"I don't know, Majesty," I answered, "but this is how it feels, isn't it?"

"Yes," she said. "This is how it feels."

Trying to coax the child to speak was exceedingly difficult, for she simply refused. As I was the one who had found her, I was always asked to be present when the wise men of court tried to snake from her indelible muteness a sound that would gain them glory or position, perhaps an embassy in a place even more remote than the wilds from which Ipwog Tookisheim had sprung with many servants, shining silver bottles, catfish-leather suitcases, and frilly embroidered shirts.

Why did they think that the sprinkling of fetid waters or the burning of rare dried moss would — any more than rubbing her hand on special royal pigs or dressing her in saffron cloth — make her identify what had driven her forth? And, as in the preparations for a ball, when love of tartan, satin, pearls, and patent leather overcomes the modest, the sensible, and the true, all the wise men of court suddenly became detectives.

They cast her footprints, cooked cloth from her dress, examined her like physicians, and declared that microscopic lines in her teeth meant that her diet included a particular kind of hard and tiny seed grown only in a certain region of the Balkash steppes, where the horsemen wore round and pointy hats and all children past the age of three had a tiny golden lion tattooed upon the wrist. That she had no such adornment proved, they said, that she was the child of outcasts or rebels, or perhaps of royal blood. But others said, no, it was because her skin was unable to take the golden ink, a condition they dubbed royal golden ink dermal rejectivist floptitis. But none of this made her speak, and meanwhile messengers were sent, and couriers, and scouts, to the prince and his armies near the Veil of Snows. But not a single one of them returned, and when nothing is heard from thousands of men in a dangerous place, everyone wonders.

The queen, however, remained confident. She had seen her husband swallowed by the mist, which had then receded and shown him still standing, as if nothing had happened. "Do you know how certain of my subjects," she asked, "run off the highest cliffs with dart-like kites, and float without fear? In that way, he takes the movement of the Veil of Snows. Its blinding edges do not impress him, and he has crossed swords in oblivion with the Golden Horde."

Still, no word arrived, and the messengers, couriers, and scouts all failed to return. Nothing seemed amiss except everything. The girl in the battered rowell was the only one who had come from beyond the city in many a month, and she was paralyzed with fear. Then, one day, after watching a nitwit philosopher show her pictures of the constellations in hope of reading the mystery in her eyes, I called for Bulgis Tookisheim.

"Sir," he said insolently when brought into my presence. "Is it the state of emergency that roused me from my bed?" Of all the Tookisheims, Bulgis was the most pompous.

"Your grace graced his bed in the afternoon?" I asked.

"Tookisheims are of noble blood, and sleep without pandering to the light."

"Bulgis," I said quietly, but firmly, "if you don't want to see your noble blood escape from your melonlike body, you will go to one of your warehouses and bring me a painting of the usurper."

"I have no such thing," he said, coyly.

244

"You have hundreds of such things. They aren't illegal, just out-moded. Bring me one. I'm requisitioning it."

"Do you want him as a scholar? Healer? Man of science? Philosopher? Explorer? Poet? Musician?"

"I want him," I interrupted, "as a killer of innocents."

"We don't have that, of course."

"It is what he would call a warrior."

"On horseback, or standing with sword?"

"Either one will do."

Bulgis disappeared quite suddenly and was back just as fast. His warehouses and depositories were everywhere, even around the corner. A nauseating oil painting of the usurper dressed for battle was brought into the room where the philosopher was still hectoring the patient child with astronomical patterns. Even though she was headed in our direction across a sea of marble, I did not wait for the queen's judgment, for I knew she would be too kind.

Two solid and compassionate varlets set the portrait in front of the child, and she turned her head to look. As the hectoring philosopher watched unmoved, she held herself stock still for a moment that proved to be the last instant of the old era. Then she screamed, doubled over, and sobbed, as everything she had held in came rushing out. I lifted her into my arms. "The usurper has returned from beyond the Veil of Snows," I said, though I did not have to say it. "And even now as we sit here doing nothing, he is conquering and killing."

Every man, woman, and child in every city, village, and remote outpost, knew that if a single one of them resisted, the usurper would kill them all. Such immense back pressure created a paralyzing

reluctance to move in one's own defense. Because the usurper wanted the village councils to be terrified and aggrieved, he would often kill even those who surrendered. He wanted someone in every village to stand and say, "If we throw ourselves down hard enough at his feet, perhaps he will spare us."

"How shall we defend ourselves?" the queen asked, as her infant slept on her lap, his tiny mouth half open, his soft limbs and little hands splayed relaxedly across the golden cloths in which he was wrapped.

"Madam, you yourself led the armies in one brilliant stroke after another to defeat the usurper. I am just a singer of tales and a common soldier, who, at the time of your victories, was chained to the wall in the Bukonsky Prison."

"I was a girl," she said, "burning with the spirit of God to conquer or defend. All was by instinct and inspiration, and nothing was to lose. Seeing this, my generals followed close on, and we had behind us the energy and anger of a kingdom oppressed for generations.

"But now the generals are old, the people have no grievance, and I have him," she said, smiling upon the beautiful child. "He has softened my heart and made me vulnerable to fear. If I am afraid for him, I cannot make the unflinching decisions that lead to victory. "

"But you must."

She smiled. "I can't."

"But why me, Majesty?"

"Why you? This is why." She held up a yellowing manuscript that I had not seen in many years. "The usurper had it here, among his things," she said. "It is your tale of the siege of Vashtan Tseloe. Never have I seen tactics as brilliant, a battle more illuminating, or a fight more real. And it came from you."

"Madam, it was just a tale. I haven't commanded anything more than a company of your guard."

The queen replied, "Every battle is a story written by its victor. The skills of a general and a teller of tales are much the same: how to judge a man's character, and where to put him in the line; what to strengthen, and what to neglect; how to cross a field of many paths; how to impress a skeptical enemy and lead followers who want to believe; how to judge the terrain, know the weather, and use the light; how to marshall all the many details for want of which a battle can be lost; and, above all, how to move an army forward like a song. I trust you to defend the city, and you must not let it fall."

"But why not Astrahn? No general is greater than Astrahn!"

"I've sent Astrahn with three armies to hold Bulgatia. If Bulgatia falls, not even Astrahn could defend the capital. The other generals are good at what they do, but have neither the freshness nor the imagination to defend a city that, like ours, is nearly indefensible.

"If my husband returns with his armies all will be well. Until that time, use what we have here. Find a way," she said, "to save this child, and the kingdom that someday will be his." She held her baby in the air, and, truly, he looked like an angel.

For a moment I stood still, trying to marshall my strength. I could not refuse my sovereign's order, and would not. For, in truth, I loved her, as did we all, but unlike most others I had the delight of looking closely upon her face and into her eyes. This feeling, like that of a young man in love, I attributed then to her royal grace and my unflagging loyalty, for I was so much older, and love, I assumed, was no longer open to me.

We heard a commotion in the reception rooms that led to her chamber. What this could be we did not know, for ordinarily no one

dared disturb her. But then Notorincus rushed in, breathlessly, after just the pretense of a knock. The queen's eyes narrowed in anger.

"Oh your majesty," he said, "a messenger has come from the Veil of Snows. He says he will say nothing to anyone except you."

I saw the queen straighten into almost a military bearing. Her mouth quivered slightly, and she breathed deeply to calm herself. "Bring him in," she said, and as Notorincus left to get the messenger, a knight whom she had known from many battles, she glanced out the window at a kingdom that was still hers. She smiled the saddest smile I have ever seen.

In the colors of the prince's army — black armor with red sash, but now stained with blood and soil — the knight limped in, back straight, visage dark and stormy.

"Report," she ordered, as of old, but with the child in her arms.

He went down on bended knee, bowed, and straightened. "Majesty," he said. "Four months it took me to make the transit from the Veil of Snows. The usurper and his multitudes have sealed the land. They rest upon it like locusts. I was captured twice, and I escaped twice. I rode on the stray horses of the dead, and in empty boats on rivers of blood. The situation in Bulgatia — "

"What of my husband, and the armies?" the queen interrupted.

"Do you not know?" the knight asked in surprise and pity.

"No," she answered, gently. "Tell me."

He then spoke what may have been the harshest words of his life. "Madam," he said, "your husband is dead, long ago, and the armies defeated. Most were killed, a few are prisoners, and perhaps some, like me, are still in the fight, but all is lost."

The queen closed her eyes and held the child tightly to her, and tears rolled down her cheeks.

"At the head of an army so vast that it blotted out the snow fields, the usurper burst from the Veil of Snows like a sudden storm. First to ride out against him was the prince. They fought as the Veil of Snows swept close, as it had done before, but this time the usurper had grown in power. It was as if he were very much larger, as if, wherever he had been, he had found stunning and inexplicable powers. He threw the prince upon the snow and struck him with his sword.

"We couldn't see any blood, for the prince's colors are red and we were at a distance, but the mists came at great speed, the usurper stepped back, and your husband, who did not move, was taken from this world."

As the queen cried, I looked out upon the city I was charged to defend, and though it lay under a tranquil blue sky in warm afternoon light, I saw before me a picture of grief and longing. How innocent and sad are beautiful things that are about to fall.

With no expectation of victory I set about nonetheless to defend, driven by duty, defiance, and the love of queen and country. The city was, indeed, almost indefensible. On low ground that sloped to the lake, its back to the water, of immense size but long and thin as it stretched along the shore, dependent for food and materiel upon a hinterland that our weakened armies were no longer large enough to protect, it cried to be abandoned. We might have made a much better fight in the mountains, from village to village, from defile to defile.

But here were the royal palace, the ancient streets and parks, the great squares, the fountains, Ferris wheels, museums, and commercial districts that are the heart of a kingdom, even if its people are hypno-

tized and enervated by color boxes and do not frequent such places anymore. Let us say that their souls are not dead, just sleeping, and that someday they will awaken to the beauty and grace of what is tranquil and Godly.

I had no time to reflect as I planned the defense. We could only guess when the assault would come, but were sure the usurper was saving us for last. Then the capital would be besieged by terrified armies of slaves fighting as slaves for the principle of slavery, and all in the currency of fear. Our estimate that we had three or four months in which to fortify was right, and had we not that much time to prepare, the city would have collapsed as soon as the enemy army darkened the plain.

The queen spoke to the assembled populace in a voice that carried miraculously high and far. When the usurper speaks to the people he uses megaphones, horns, and repeaters (little fat-men who stand on boxes and instantly relay his words down long lines of frightened citizens). And his words themselves are the work of a team that spends a month destroying the simplicity of a fifteen-minute speech. His phrases leave him like shot falling upon the crowd. When the queen spoke, however, she would just stand and speak, and her easily flowing words — wise, sagacious, and chaste — left her like doves thrown to fly.

What she said was very simple. Though the enemy was quite terrifying, death itself, she was reconciled and calm, and would defy him until the very last. Anyone who chose self-preservation by exiting the city would be allowed to do so, but after five days, when the work of defiance had begun, those who went over to the other side would be executed. Bulgatia was holding, and messengers had been sent to Dolomitia-Swift to beg the help of this just kingdom whose armies had never known defeat. "I myself will not leave," she said. "With my son, who someday will be king, I will either perish or prevail in your midst."

Though a few trickled out the gates, it was best to be rid of them, for those that remained were solid and true. Then I gathered soldiers, engineers, physicians, politicians, and provisioners, and we started on the design. Our first problem was water. Even had we built cisterns the snowfall would not have been enough to sustain us: we had to continue drawing from the lake. The difficulty was that the inlet pipes were far from land and beyond cannon shot. As they were not so deep that our divers had been unable to build them, they were not so deep that the usurper's divers could not seal them shut. For this we had a remedy, an Archimedean hammer that would send explosive pressure through water, an incompressible medium, to pop any cap like a champagne cork. But after one or two tries this might easily destroy the entire conduit. We hadn't the time and it was the wrong season in which to build new inlets.

So we built a reservoir in the palace square, with walls of marine oak and every gap caulked including the spaces between the cobbles. The bulkheads were almost as high as a man, and the area flooded so vast that in it we could keep enough water to last for two years. To keep the water aerated and fresh, fifty windmills turned waterwheels that each lifted a score of immense troughs, emptying into chutes that combed the water into white foam. These did not work when the wind blew feebly, but in a squall the reservoir boiled as forcibly as sugar.

The cross walls that divided it into many lakes were not to strengthen it (for there is no more pressure on a wall holding back a given height of water if the water is as extensive as the ocean or just a hand's breadth across) but to stop wind-driven waves that with a silken rolling resonance might very well have smashed the timbers and flooded every lower floor in the city.

Our second problem was food. The old emperor had built storage structures and granaries sufficient to feed the city for five years (and the mice for five thousand). We would lack only dairy products, fresh vegetables, and fruit. To remedy this I called in the architects. "I want to know," I said, "exactly how much weight the flat portions of the palace and state roofs can hold." They reported after their surveys that the roofs were built to hold the weight of fifty consecutive snows, for construction of the palace had begun in the time of the great and unending winters, when the sun was maroon and the snow never ceased.

We hauled soil in carts and sacks, and on the rooftops we built a garden so vast you could not see the end of it in any direction. Dairy herds and flocks of sheep and goats dotted the squares of turf and brown soil. A region of orchards, carried up tree by tree, made a reddened overture to the golden autumn, but it was so far away from the queen's tower, whence I saw it, that it looked like a sparkle of sunlight.

Although I made a suggestion or two, I left to the quartermasters the task of producing the maximum number possible of cannonballs, crossbow bolts, arrows, and catapults. One especially giant machine was constructed to hurl the city's accumulated garbage onto the enemy camp. If their siege would prevent us from carting it away, we said, we would pass the baton to them, and the workers who built this machine never stopped smiling.

Though I was not a general, I created the strategy for defending the city. All the generals professed to be impressed, even those who did not habitually butter up the queen. We built sectional walls through-

out the city, just as we had done in the reservoir, and according to exactly the same rationale — to break the momentum and pressure of assaulting waves. And while we were erecting impediments we were also clearing channels and making roads that mercilessly cut through the city but that would amplify the powers of our diminished armies by allowing them to move so fast they could almost be in four places at once. Every sector had teams for reconnaissance, damage control, care of the sick and wounded, householding and supply, communications, etc. And then there were the mobile brigades, cavalry mostly, that would reinforce a weak point with overwhelming strength after galloping along the network of new roads.

That was it. We worked hard, and when it was done it was done, and we waited. In this peculiar twilight time, when so many people forgave and were reconciled to one another, we lived in a holy city that even as we moved toward winter seemed full of quickening light. As much as we could, we retired from affairs of state and things of the world. Families stayed by their fires. Courting couples became inseparable. The old became stiller yet, listening to the clocks that tick even for the young. And the queen remained most of the time in the royal apartments, alone with her son. For hour upon hour she spoke to him, though he could not understand, of chances lost and chances left, of history, hope, and courage, of his father, and of love, although of that she had hardly to say a word.

Autumn started soft and turquoise and then became sapphire and clear. The lake kicked up in white-topped boat-swamping swells; the same wind that gelled the sides of black waves stripped the trees of their orange blaze; and the falling leaves were like Greek fire on paper boats drifting through columns of cold shadow. Winter came early in December, covering the plains with the white that even in summer

257

had never strayed from the mountaintops. The snow was pleasing: we had our house in order, and the usurper's armies would have to camp on fields as hard and cold as ice.

On the twenty-ninth of December, a cruel and sunless day, a sentry at the southeast corner of the wall reported that the snow seemed to be melting, that the plain seemed to be rolling up toward us like the brown edge that moves along a burning piece of paper. This sudden thaw, we soon discovered, was the effect of the usurper's armies blotting out the snow.

Two million men covered the wintered plain until it looked like a field in May, and on the first evening their hundred thousand fires burned like stars that had stuck and flared in the raw earth. Supply trains never ceased to move in hundreds of gossamer lines disappearing over the horizon. At night their bright torches seemed to jiggle up and down. In the day and from a distance the long lines of horses and camels looked like black spider webs swaying in slow motion on the wind.

Ten thousand siege engines, many larger than our own, were brought close, and long ladders were stacked up like piles of twigs. And they were boiling oil. What for? Because we were on the walls, it was our job to pour boiling oil on them, and this was the cause of much resentment. It led the Tookisheims to claim that the usurper's men were friendly, and were merely making soup, an interpretation that was rejected after they pumped it into high-pressure hoses and squirted it over the walls in lines of flame that looked like dragon pee.

And, with their machines, what did they throw at the walls and into the city? What did they *not* throw? Boulders, of course, and every other kind of rock; bombs; bladders of flaming oil; cannonballs; sharpened chains that whizzed through the air and decapitated steeples; dead animals infected with plague; lead pellets that routinely broke every window in the city; crazed fighting jackals that descending under silken canopies, bit themselves free upon landing, and then fiercely attacked anything with a pulse; and arrows, fleets of them, so that all our wooden buildings looked like porcupines in heat.

We ourselves worked hard showering the enemy with projectiles and flames, and after a month or two it began to feel like the ordinary state of things. As the usurper's ships prowled the lake, we turned to the reservoir, which, because of all the churning, did not freeze. We were optimistic of survival, though we realized that our opponents had not made their first charge, had not broken into the city, and had yet to breach the wall.

The first attempt came on a frozen night in February. We watched as two million soldiers dressed for battle. These were our own people, fighting sadly against us, but ferociously, and when the first blow came the city almost collapsed upon itself.

From a crescent of ten thousand archers, arrows would flow in a continuous stream toward one narrow point, at which the siege engines and ten to twenty towers would slowly move. Nothing could be done, no oil poured, no arrows or shot rained down upon them, because of the covering fire that made it impossible even to peek over the battlements. In this way, they breached the wall in fifty places, positioning ten or twenty stair towers, and a hundred flimsy ladders in between. In a few minutes, a thousand men would pour into a single breach, so that within the space of half an hour, they had fifty thousand men within the walls, with hundreds of thousands lined up behind them ready to follow.

We channeled each penetration by keeping strong pressure on it from left and right, and that day three hundred thousand enemy soldiers were forced into terrible battles in the narrow streets. Though it was my own plan, I shuddered to think of its effect. Five thousand of the usurper's soldiers, screaming havoc and death, would charge down a street only wide enough for two wagons. When they had surged as far as their numbers could support, and had begun to slow with doubt, we lowered a gate in front of them. Now they were in a tight pen, trapped between the gate before them and the battlements behind.

By the thousand — for we, too, had armies — our archers appeared in the windows and on the rooftops. The arrows flew so thickly in both directions, with hundreds colliding head on and many splitting in two, that the air looked like the sunlight space above a wild threshing floor. And when it was done, God forgive us, the only way to clear the streets of the dead was to hurl them over the wall.

We held that day and in the days after, but we lost so many soldiers and our hearts became so heavy that we began to picture defeat. Time passed very painfully. After six surges, the decimation of the armies, and the loss of half the city, we were still in winter, and it was still deadeningly cold and dark. Even the streets that were ours were unsafe: raiding parties emerged from the sewers, from over the rooftops, and from the neck of the catapults, to descend noiselessly by silken parachute. As we died slowly by degree, defeat began to rise like the sun.

Everything was in short supply — wood for fires, medicine and food, heat, arms and ammunition, human energy, and hope. By every measure, as we became weaker, the enemy grew stronger, until we began to wonder if perhaps we deserved our fate, if God had ceased to favor us and now looked kindly upon our foe.

By mid-March, as the sun grew stronger over land still covered in snow, we had lost two-thirds of the city, including the reservoir. The loyal, the faithful, and those who were barely alive had taken refuge in the palace. Now under the usurper's law, the city took to life in the regimented fashion of the previous regime. The markets were active once again. The streetcars ran. Soldiers in neat ranks rode silently on the Ferris wheels.

Sometime in March — I don't remember when, for I was too tired to make sense of time — we heard a great roar from without the palace walls. We thought this was the cheer before the final assault, for they had been so thoroughly marshalling their forces and building so many engines and towers that they would have to come at us only one time. It was to have been an overwhelming blow, and the more their preparations continued within our sight, the harder it was for us to maintain our flagging will to fight.

But it was not the cheer before an assault, it was a shout of victory. Bulgatia had fallen, Astrahn was dead, the armies in chains. We, then, were the only ones left. Against the usurper's reinforced and replenished armies we could throw just a hundred thousand men, half of whom were sick and the other half dizzy with hunger.

And yet the queen would not surrender. She was not born to surrender, and for that we loved her, though we were certain we were about to fall. She was splendid then, even if her mind sometimes wandered, even if she sometimes seemed distracted, and even if she spoke to her child of his father as if the father still lived. Perhaps this was the price she paid for being resolute in the face of the enemy. "Defy them," she said to her trembling army, weak even from lack of water. "Defy them. For now that we have nothing, defiance is all."

263

In early spring come the winds that signal breakup of the ice. And though the surface of the lake remains as solid as if it will last forever, the snow blows across it in cold lines of blue that mimic ice fractured in the sun. From the city the armies of air passing over the lake seemed both mysterious and terrible. What animates such frigid air? What gives it power and velocity? And to what battle is it directed with such apparent resolve that it makes of drifts of snow nothing more than stunned arrows pointing to where it has disappeared?

When all but the queen were reconciled to die, when we felt as if we knew the wind and where it was going, and were no longer afraid to think of going with it, the Duke of Tookisheim's purple carriage rolled up to the palace gates and waited for permission to enter, which, after a time, was granted.

As they made their way toward the royal apartments, he and his retainers looked out of their gilt-framed windows of deep gray glass and saw the faces of our soldiers. Not the soundproofing of his carriage but the absolute silence of our men rattled the Duke of Tookisheim, who could not believe that, because he himself would not, anyone else could fight beyond all calculation, all advantage, and all prospect of victory. We fought not for victory or advantage, but because the fighting as we lasted became a song that we did not want to stop singing, and it was that song itself that gave us life. No wonder the Duke of Tookisheim could not understand. All he and his kind could do was calculate, something at which we, alas, had proved not too skilled.

We led him into the queen's presence, and this was a sight to see, our almost emaciated sovereign who would eat only the rations of a common soldier, and the Duke of Tookisheim, swollen like a hog's bladder floating down a stream in the hot sun. She, delicate and thin, her lovely chestnut hair floating about skin as smooth as ivory, and he, florid, pitted, and bewigged. She, with thin tortoise-shell spectacles, smelling of roses, voice chastened by defeat. He, in spectacles of snake-colored metal with sequined scales, smelling of octopus and marmalade (his breakfast), voice like a calliope and beating drum. She, a hundred and twenty pounds. He, two hundred and seventy. She, with eyes in which floated worlds. He, with the eyes of a fish late to market.

"What is it, Tookisheim?" she asked, abandoning formalities.

"Majesty!" he answered, with the sarcasm of a cat who is polite to a mouse. "Have you had enough to eat?"

"Not by your standards," she replied.

"I beg your pardon?"

"Not if one measures lunch in octopuses."

"Octopuses, Majesty, or, as the scholars might say, octo-*pies*, are a breakfast food."

"Whole?" asked the queen.

The Duke of Tookisheim's face became almost angelic as he said, "When stuffed with marmalade, asparagus, and lemon chiffon."

"Thank you for making me happy that I have hardly eaten in the last six months. I would not have thought it would be possible."

"Delighted," he said, bowing slightly, fake birthmark twitching.

"Well? What do you want? You have moved from the place where you were to the place where you are. You don't do that except if you want something."

"Would you care to surrender?" he asked. "No one will be executed except you and your child. The others will be spared, I think."

At first we were as stunned as if a bomb had just exploded and we had been visited with the customary paralysis. But then we unfroze.

"No!" shouted a soldier who would not otherwise have dared speak to his queen. She forgave him, it seemed, perhaps because she herself had not known what to say. Had the price been her death alone, she would immediately have accepted it. But not even to save hundreds of thousands of her subjects would a woman see her child murdered. It simply is not written that way, and never will be.

And our queen, whose heart went out to the fathers and sons who manned her armies, all of them mothers' children, was broken by this, and remained speechless. I joined in the insubordination, I too said "no," and the same word soon followed with absolute conviction from every man in the room. The queen looked at Tookisheim, as if in amazement, and said, "My husband, when he returns from the Veil of Snows, will thrash you." In that moment, I wanted desperately to embrace her, and in that moment some of the soldiers bent their heads in pity.

Then two sergeants grabbed Tookisheim and dragged him out, bumping his bulk down the steps and throwing him back into his purple carriage, which bounced so hard on its springs that the retainers were thrown against the frescoed ceiling and the jingling of their necklaces and jewels sounded like a box of sleigh bells thrown down the stairs of a steeple.

That was when the queen laughed at first, and then, pivoting toward me, cried for all the terrible things to come. And that was when I took her into my arms, for although I was only a soldier, and women hesitated even to look upon me, and she was my sovereign, there was no one else. Perhaps nothing is as strong or fine as unrequited love when by discipline it is kept properly in its place, but I'm glad that, for this short time, I held her, as delicately as ever I could, for it had been so long since anyone had, and it was the last time that anyone would.

266

Those of us who remained seemed to realize simultaneously that for standing fast in the palace itself we would be hunted through the darkness of its lowest labyrinths, and we could not see ourselves, much less our lovely queen, hiding in bins of rotted feed with the rats, or emerging with whitened eyes from the dust of coal chutes to engage small detachments of the usurper's armies in increasingly futile engagements.

"We can't escape across the lake," the queen said to her generals, "as we don't have enough boats, and even if we did they would be sunk, for we long ago gave up the navy, thinking that we didn't need a navy on a lake that was entirely our own. And if we had the boats and if we had a navy, and reached the other side, where would we go? The only direction in which to flee would take us to Bulgatia."

We all knew what she had in mind, and that she wanted us to think of it ourselves, so we did.

"Is there any hope?" she asked. "In what direction can we turn?"

"The mountains, Majesty," said a wizened general from the time of the old emperor, a white-haired ancient with mustaches like clouds. "Only in the mountains do we have a chance."

The queen straightened and her eyes seemed less filled with sadness, for the mountains were where she had spent her girlhood, raised by the royal tutor who she had thought was her grandfather, and where eventually she had learned that she, a simple girl with no pretenses, was the rightful queen. That she had come down to the plain not to avenge her murdered forebears but to keep faith with them was nothing less than the history of us all. And now that she wanted to go back, it seemed right, just right, exactly so, for as you fall you reach for what you love and what you know.

The old general continued. "There," he said, "we will have the limitless space in which to dilute any number of the usurper's pursuing forces until they will have to face us one by one. There, if we can reach it, is a place where our children may find shelter, anonymity, and peace."

"The mountains," said the queen, gravely, for she knew the price.

"If . . ." the general went on, "if we reach them alive, we cannot fail to have left behind at least a half of all who exit the city. The fight to reach the foothills may take ninety of a hundred soldiers, or we may fail to break through. Still, I cannot imagine that a single one of your soldiers, or any of their families, would prefer to die here rather than in the open air."

"We can't poll them," the queen said. "There is no time, and if there were, the spies would give us away."

"When we break out," the general confirmed, "it must be with no more than an hour of preparation. Some will enter the grates and tunnels knowing only then what has been decided."

"If we march out straight," Notorincus said, "they'll attack us from both sides and ahead. Our column will be like a strudel in a room full of rats."

I then remembered my role as strategist. Although I could not claim to have broken the siege, we were still alive, and in war that is a fine credential. "We'll go east," I said, "using the lake to protect our northern flank, and the city the western. Toward the east the enemy's sparse deployments stop five minutes' ride from the battlements. He'll turn everything he has from the plain to attack our southern flank, which, of necessity, will be long. But his armies will choke into slow-moving columns as he tries to reach us, and the effect of their overwhelming numbers will be lessened. Our archers and pikemen will defend the long column of march as best they can, while our cavalry runs parallel to our route, breaking up the attacking fronts on the perpendicular, like a knife cutting bread."

"And then we'll turn," the queen said. "That is, what is left of us, and go south to the mountains. After how many days of fighting will we have broken free enough to change direction?"

"Three or four," the generals said. This was the kind of thing they knew.

"And what are our chances?" the queen asked.

"It is likely," replied the old general, knowing that he himself would never see steep white mountains over dark blue meadows, "that some will get through. A hundred, perhaps, or twenty."

No matter the severity of the old man's estimate, we left the city on the warmest evening of late March, when the enemy had stood his weapons and was three-quarters of the way through a heavy dinner. An hour of sunlight and dusk, and it would be dark.

The eastern flank of the besieging armies had been denuded to bring its best troops into the city for the attack on the palace, and what remained was placed under the command of Staveetz Tookisheim, a rarity in the Tookisheim tribe both because he was a military man and because he did not share the Tookisheim predilections for sloth, filth, indolence, vanity, inanity, and idiocy.

Though a third of their force was comprised of siege engines pointed haplessly toward the battlements, they still outnumbered us five to one in foot soldiers and cavalry, and had great stocks of arrows and shot, which we did not, and they had eaten. In fact, though their recently filled stomachs would slow them in battle, we who were hungry, lithe, and fast envied them for eating even if they were condemned to the Tookisheim diet of fried everything: fried salad, fried apples, fried syrup, fried salt — fried, fried, everything fried — fried

water, and fried milk. And all the fried water that they were served at meals was flavored with the batter-fried ink of fried octopuses and squids. What a family, what a clan, what a cuisine.

Our first wave of cavalry burst out of half a dozen secret tunnels spread along the route of escape. From the farthest exit beyond the enemy lines, a thousand horsemen left a fold in the ground and grouped to charge west into the setting sun. At the same time, other thousands appeared, some even from beneath the enemy tents, lifting them like ghosts, and they began to fight along axes of least resistance designed to stun Staveetz's command and split his army into broken sections.

After half an hour of this our five easternmost gates were opened and from each poured two thousand cavalry galloping forth and then reversing direction to create a wall of horsemen behind which the main body could travel along the lakeshore.

At the center of the main body I was with the queen and her personal guard. The infant rode in an upright cradle that hung across the saddle of a strong charger. In his cloths of gold he was then placed in a soft and comfortably padded chamber overhung by a slanting roof of wood and leather. Although he could see out, neither rain nor missiles could get in, and the frame of the little box was strong enough so that even were the charger to roll on his side it would not be crushed. Carried with him, wrapped, as was he, in golden cloth, were pages written by the queen to tell him of what had come before. She of all people knew that the saddest thing in the world was for a parent to have his child loosed upon the wing, and that of this she stood a good chance. And yet she was unperturbed, for her own parents were as alive in her heart as if she had known them, and perhaps more so.

She was dressed for battle in her customary way, with a light bow, a small sword, and not that many arrows. Though her child was shield-ed, she wore no armor. It was her duty to be exposed, because her sol-diers would be incalculably vigilant and hardfighting if they knew she was among them, in a rain of arrows, with neither plate nor mail. I, too, wore neither plate nor mail, out of deference to her, and because I could not stand the thought that a shower of crossbow bolts would take her life and leave me unscathed. My sword, however, was a full sword, and my quiver heavy with the strongest arrows. I also held a short lance, the end butted to a cup in my saddle.

For hours we moved forward without the necessity of counter-attack, so thoroughly had we rattled our opponents, who wasted half their strength thrusting through the palace gates, only to find no one inside. We suffered many casualties, though mainly in the cavalry, for the enemy was not alert enough to launch arrows at the scores of thousands who proceeded in back of this shield. Even the old general with the whitened hair was suddenly possessed with new energy as he saw our vast column break out of the enemy cordon days ahead of schedule.

Messengers seeking out our banners arrived in a constant stream, and from one of them we learned of our luck. He arrived just as we were reforming the column to take the blow expected from the south. No one had dared to imagine that the usurper would not wheel his hosts in a semicircle to strike us broadside. But the messenger told us that the usurper had become ill, evidently from something that he had eaten.

Most wonderfully, the Duke of Tookisheim had been given com-mand, an astonishing lapse attributable mainly to the usurper's nau-sea. Even Peanut must have been shaken to see his father take control of the armies as he did. The duke's purple carriage carried him to a platform on the southwest wall, where he directed the battle with the aid of semaphores and brass telescopes, all the while distracted by a six-hour picnic laid upon linen-covered outdoor tables, many of which would have collapsed from the weight of the champagne bottles standing upon them had he not done his duty in drinking them down to reduce the strain.

The first thing he did, which accounted for our unexpectedly quick passage, was to give a hell-and-thunder speech about crème caramel. His troops, lined up by the hundred thousand, could hardly hear what he was saying, and could hardly see the chef's utensils he brandished like a trial lawyer, but they were only too happy to stay out of the battle. And who but the Duke of Tookisheim could talk with passion, hysteria, and tears about cremè caramel for six hours straight, throwing in a homily here and there about the subtleties of fried octopus?

When at last he decided to attack, he had them storm the vacant palace, where he lost half of them in the infinite maze of rooms, halls, and galleries. If I know soldiers, and I do, many a patrol was ended in a featherbed in one of the innumerable apartments, as a hardwood blaze heated what had been drinking water in a shiny nickel apparatus for the bath, and the rich oriental carpets grew ever more lustrous in maturing firelight reflected from cherry paneling.

Completely flummoxed and still gallantly reducing the weight on the suffering picnic tables, the Duke of Tookisheim called for a harpsichord, and when it was brought to him he sat down at it and began to play and sing. This got his blood up, and he shouted out orders to charge. From having witnessed various court entertainments he knew enough of technicalities to get his cavalry going, but most of them he sent either back into the city, stupefied at the walls, or galloping into the lake.

Those ordered to us, randomly, did not wheel from the south but were directed at our rear guard on an extremely narrow front. It was like holding a bridge. Fifty thousand cavalry charged east, but they contacted us only in a line of ten or twenty. The fighting was bitter and their supply of replacements seemingly endless, but they could not even dent our position. This went on through the night, and by midmorning of the next day we found ourselves, still intact, near the foothills.

The queen ordered a counterattack upon the pursuing column, and we wheeled broadside and struck them from two directions at once, breaking them up so decisively that all the forces of what now was the state retreated to regroup. In this lull, ninety thousand of us who were still alive gathered around a windblown knoll to hear the queen speak.

The breeze was soft and the snow melting as she spoke, the great horses in back of her ready to run to new places and graze in unimagined fields. Her voice somehow carried, as it always did, with the wind bringing it as if by magic to every ear. First she looked over the remnants of her kingdom, who stood in unaccountable comfort beneath luffing banners and a pale blue sky.

"Thank God we have been spared. And spared we have been," she said. "In a moment, my kingdom and yours will cease to exist, for here and now it must come to an end, and from here we will scatter to the mountains to protect our lives. There, ahead, against the Veil of Snows, you will find infinite space for healing, and there, if there is a God, my son will find his father. You will not always be free from the usurper's edicts and impressments. It will all depend upon where you go, how fast you move, and the nature of your luck. All I ask is that you remember. Why, I do not know, except perhaps to love and honor those who are lost, those who, in dying, were robbed of the story ahead—unless my fondest hopes are real.

275

"Scatter to the far corners of this land, hide on mountainsides and in dells, settle by fast-flowing streams and in the deep sheltering silence of the forest. Scatter, and remember, and perhaps someday our children's children will remember, and faint memories will swell into the fires that will guide them home."

And then, as was her custom, she did not wait to see others do her bidding, but quickly mounted, followed by her guard, who flew into their saddles as if it was not a day of defeat. She cast one last gentle smile back at the silent thousands, took the reins of the charger that carried her son, and spurred her horse.

I do not know what was said or felt as we left, but soon we found ourselves in silence but for the horses' breathing, the sound of hoof-beats, and the creaking of saddlery. We passed streams that had cut through the snow, and flowers that had burst from it, and we made for a faraway crest beyond which seemed to be a world of clouds, a luminous line of red and gold floating above a range of dark hills.

In the queen's guard was a young soldier who, just as we were breaking free, was badly wounded by the kind of arrow that is launched from a catapult. With a heavy shaft and a blunt head, it is designed for breaking fortifications. Though when he fell he begged the queen to leave him, she would not, and from then on he traveled with us, lying on a frame slung between two yoked-together horses. As this slowed our pace, most of the other mounted detachments disappeared ahead of us into the hills, splaying out in many directions and always pulling away.

After the second day in the foothills we were running and rising in steep forests and over huge plateaux still snow covered but for an

276

occasional newly greening field. The wounded boy could no longer speak. Though we knew he would die we dared not stop, for great armies were following our many tracks, and our only hope was to keep moving either until the strengthening sun obliterated our trail in the snow or we entered regions so remote, so crossed by rivers, so rocky, vast, and steep, that we would simply disappear, inexplicably and in peace.

On the third or perhaps the fourth or fifth night — I cannot remember — we halted on a huge table of rock over which ran shallow streams heated by the sun until the water was hot. And the rock itself, hot and dry, was a welcome change from thawing ground and melted snow.

As soon as we dismounted we started fires and set up kettles of water that, already heated, boiled fast. We tended the dying soldier, took care of the horses, and ate what little we had to eat as the dry wood blazed, the stars came out, and the streams ran in the dark. We were twenty all told, and after we had rested a little we sent out a captain to backtrack and stand guard. If he placed himself well he would hear the approach of horses or see them against even the night sky as they crested a ridge and briefly obliterated bright stars. This was one of the skills of soldiering beyond those of battle. It was floating on the current rather than thrashing against it.

When in early morning the captain returned from his night watch he told us that our track was marked by widely separated spots of blood. Only once every half hour or so, he said, but as regular as a stitch. The blood had come from the wounded boy, whose strength, we hoped, might still carry him through, although our judgment was that it would not.

"What does it matter?" the queen asked. "We always leave the compacted tracks of twenty horses, indelible upon rock, lasting for weeks in soft earth and for days or more in snow."

"The tiny drops of blood, Majesty," replied the captain, "probably stretch all the way to the knoll, where we left many of our banners, and where, with only slight consideration, the enemy would place your speech to our army before it scattered. The hoofprints of our horses would have been lost amid the hundreds of thousands that chopped the snow in that place as the army broke up and followed us. But any good tracker should be able to disentangle our path from all the others by following the scarlet trace. We are not safe."

"And when will we be safe?" the queen asked.

"Only when he stops bleeding or is left behind."

"We don't leave our wounded behind," the queen said, "even if they are heroes who beg for it."

"Even if it may lead to the death of your child?"

The queen lifted her head almost like an animal catching a scent, and she said, "Yes, even if it may lead to that."

"It means that we must ride slowly," the captain told her, eyes cast down, "while our pursuers ride fast."

These were hardly easy times for the queen, but she only grew in her graces. "You have observed deer, Captain, have you not? You have even hunted them?"

"Yes, Majesty."

"So have I observed them. They are born to be hunted and pursued, and they are born defenseless. I watched in the forest when I was a girl, and then, later, after I had become queen, and my nobles hunted them. All they can do is run, and they do, but many of them are taken. How is it, do you suppose, that they can live, knowing this, knowing that at any time their children can be cut down, or they

themselves, leaving children alone in the world? How is it, Captain, that, knowing this, they can live?"

"I don't know, Majesty. I only hunted them. I did not put myself in their place."

"Now you are in their place."

"Yes."

"And now you must do as they do."

"Be nervous, Majesty?"

She laughed. "No, not nervous, but alert. And grateful. Let all sensation thunder in, stay with those you love, and trust in the time you have left."

And then, knowing that our time was marked, we mounted and rode on, lifted by love and defiance, listening to all sound, galloping toward mountains and light.

In the high country of this kingdom the light deepens, confuses, and protects. Mountainsides that from a distance might look flat are ennobled by light and shadow that give them dark and precipitous clefts and roll the summits like windblown clouds. The light will vary in such a way that valleys once colliding will seem to run apart, and vast calderas, like patches upon the ocean, drift from places thought fixed.

I do not know how many days we rode, or weeks or months, for it was easy to lose track of time in the light and lovely colors, and in the hundred miles of deep blue. We hardly spoke as we moved through forests somnolent in eternal peace, past sparkling lakes enclosed by rings of purple granite. The insistent motion of our horses driving ever deeper into God's country was a steadily building song that we dared not interrupt. We would stop at dusk, and after eating and washing would fall into the kind of sleep that knits together the strengths of the next day. And then we were off before sunrise, rising hour by hour into the increasingly sharp air.

The boy did not die until early one afternoon when we stopped by the shallows of a cold river that shone in the sun. The last thing he knew was the clean smell of waters newly born from ice, and then he left us. We used the water boiling above our fires to prepare him for burial, and set about digging a grave in the chalky soil under a little bluff where we had taken shelter from the wind.

As the sun reflected almost blindingly from the river and the rock it was warm there, and I was resting, when the queen approached me. I began to stand so that I could sink to one knee, but she signaled me to stay. She sat on a boulder behind me and to the right, where, if I were looking straight ahead, I could not see her. The baby was sleeping in its cradle on the horse, which grazed on wet grass that came up between the river-polished rocks. With eighteen soldiers left, the kingdom that once had been ours seemed only like a dream.

"Now they won't even have a trail of blood to follow," she said, with regret. "Do you think they're close?"

"I don't know," I replied over the sound of the waters, "but they would have had no infant to spare on hard roads, no wounded man, and, forgive me, your grace, no queen for whom one's regard leads to what might have been fatal courtesy."

She was astonished. "I thought we were riding as hard as we could."

"Oh no ma'am," I said, my deep love for her contained within me by sad and perfect discipline. "Had we left the boy behind, we could have ridden much harder, much faster, and used up more of the nights. We might have worn out some horses, but we would have gone twice as far. We would never, my dear lady, have stopped for a midday meal."

"We must ride like that now," she said, "until we go so deeply into these mountains that we can never be found."

"They're following the trail now, Majesty, not the blood, but we'll move faster."

"I'll feed the baby as I ride. I've done it already."

"Yes."

"I want to drive so deep that when finally we stop we'll have no idea of what is real."

I nodded, thinking of what had once been unthinkable, of passing the rest of my life with this young queen, and watching her age, while living at the edge of a glacier and by a full speeding stream, of becoming the old man who would instruct the young prince in what he lost and how to retrieve it, of pipes and flutes that echoed in the farthest valleys, of years of fires sweet and hot in darkness crowned by the ice of stars.

"But shall we not leave now?" she asked, for there was something about that bluff, where the stream took a slight turn onto a high plain at the foot of mountains that we guessed to be the highest of any that were. Beyond them, we thought, were lower and gentler lands more remote than any we had ever dreamed of.

"We'll ride as soon as the boy is buried. Those mountains may be the last and highest range."

"I want to see the forests that no one has ever seen," she said. "I want my son to grow up where the green is infinite and there is no time."

"Time will mean nothing to him."

"And he will remember nothing of the city that was," she said.

"Ma'am, when I was young I lived with my mother and father in a house near the march-lands. It was modest but beautiful, and as a child I imagined that it would always last."

"Has it?"

"'I don't know. I've never been back, but when I first came to the capital, in the time of your grandfather, I worked at building houses and discovered something sad and true. I learned that houses are delicate frames that hold people only tenuously, that walls and floors are made of weak pieces weakly stitched together, that they are broken apart by rain and snow, by gravity, and the movement of the earth. I learned that they go quickly in fire, and that windows shatter in a storm and doors are broken by enemies and those who are angry. I learned that there is no safety and no shelter in anything we can build or do, that the safest and most sheltering place is in the open, in what we call forever."

She understood, and I saw that she was content. I take comfort in that, for those moments, under the open sky by the river, were her last.

Something told me that all was not right. I turned to the grave, where the men were gathered, and counted them. They were seventeen, I was with the queen, our horses were hobbled and grazing. Out of sorrow for the boy, the sentries had come down from the bluff, and no one was watching or in the rearguard.

I stood to order them back, but before the words could leave me I heard a whistle almost like the cry of a marmot, and an arrow pierced my left shoulder from behind. When things such as this happen so much occurs at once and so quickly that time turns from water dashing across rocks to honey that will not leave the jar.

Our soldiers went for their weapons and horses, for they had turned as I stood and their eyes had been upon me as I was struck. A hundred helmets and the tips of bows bloomed from the top of the bluff that had hidden the enemy's approach, and he came from behind us as well from the side, and detachments of riders suddenly appeared across the stream.

The queen had dropped to the ground and was about to rush for her son when I told her to pull out the arrow. I would not be able to fight otherwise. In one leap she moved behind me, but then as she pulled all she did was pull me toward her. "I can't get it," she said.

"Put your foot on my back."

She did, and pulled, and as the arrow came out I fell face forward onto the rocky ground. I felt a terrible pain where the arrow had been, but I forgot my pain when I saw the queen racing to the charger through air that had become wood-colored with arrows. The archers fired fast and mechanically from all around, and as I stood I was struck by another arrow. It opened a wound in my thigh and pushed on to kill a man behind me. I knelt and drew my bow. Never had I been so concentrated, and my targets were obligingly lined up in a row. Though their arrows crisscrossed in the air, they stayed clear of me, and I knocked at least ten archers from the chalky cliff.

Half our men were already dead when the attacking cavalry rode in, swords flashing, horses breathing hard. As I dropped my bow and drew my sword I saw that the queen had mounted and was riding at full gallop toward her son. She cut the line that held his charger, brought her sword back, and struck the horse hard on the withers with the flat so that he would run, anywhere, to save the child.

Then Notorincus and another man appeared, mounted, leading my horse. They stopped only briefly, and I flew into the saddle, spurring the horse the moment I was on his back. Enemy cavalry was converging on the queen, and the charger with her infant son had been forced into the stream, where the water was up to the belly of the war horse and he went rampant to strike infantrymen who tried to kill him with pikes and swords, but who, in steady rhythm, were swept off their feet and into the current either as he struck them down or as they lost their footing on the slick rock. The river now was white and red. Blood filled the water, in pools that quickly stretched into lines as thin as ropes and thread.

As I galloped to the queen, who was on her horse, fighting in the shallows, wielding her sword against foot soldiers and cavalry, the man to my left was knocked from his saddle by an arrow. He went over the neck of the horse and died before he hit the ground, while Notorincus and I, who reached the queen, at least had the satisfaction of being mounted, armed, and at the side of our sovereign as she fought.

As her sword battered their pewter-colored armor and chain—the officers, in the color of black, had held back — she kept an eye on the charger as he was driven farther into the deepening stream. The wooden cradle repeatedly flew into the air and banged against the saddle. Half the time it was suspended in blue and the other half it was slamming against the dark leather over the dappled gray coat. As his mother fought fiercely to get to him and the baby cried, more and more men surrounded her. Even as she struck them down one after another and we cut them into pieces as if they had been apples, they crowded the river until you could hardly see the water.

A thousand men or more had been sent after us, and had persevered. Twenty men cannot fight a thousand. Two men and a woman cannot fight a thousand, even if she is a queen, and even if they love her.

I glanced at Notorincus, and before I turned away I saw him lifted from his horse by a pike. Poor Notorincus, after a flight through the air, fell and disappeared into the mass of dull armor. I turned to the queen. "Notorincus is gone," I said.

She answered silently, moving her lips. I never knew what she said. And we fought on. God knows we fought on, until the charger slipped on its side and went into the water, cradle underneath, and we could fight no longer.

The queen spurred her horse toward her son's, which, thrashing, was beginning to float downstream, but we could not move forward through the mass of men surrounding us. The queen lifted her sword and threw it at a soldier who had gripped her horse's bridle, killing him, but another jumped to his place.

Now she had no sword, now she had no arrows, someone reached up and pulled off her spectacles, and the charger was floating full in the stream. As I cut down soldier after soldier, and tried to make a channel through their ranks, she stood on the back of her horse and leapt toward the water. She landed amid a group of amazed and flattened enemy, who fell back in a ring to give her space.

I did what she had done, but as I flew toward her I was struck many times with sword and stave, and I landed at her feet, bloody and hardly able to move. We could no longer even see the deep part of the stream, and as the young queen knelt in shallow water, she put her hand on the small of my back.

"I'm sorry," she said, and she wept.

The only thing I could say, as I coughed blood, was no, no, and no again, and I kept saying no as I tried to struggle to my feet. Then an officer appeared, a young man, who ordered his men to step back to clear a view of the river.

Far down the stream we saw what looked like a round white rock moving through the rapids, drawn away from us so quickly that at first it was a spot and then it was only the memory of a spot, and then all we could see was a line of something that looked like white wool, the surface of distant roiling water.

"That was your son," the officer said to the queen, who now wanted only to die. "The story ends here."

I was lying in the bloody water, facing her, when I saw her bow her head to pray. Words would not come from me. I had to move. I knew I could not fight, but I had nothing else to do but try. And then I saw a huge sword rise in the air behind her.

Our lives are not what we think. They are cut down not at our will, and extended not at our will, as was mine, thank God, though at the time this was not what I had wanted, not after what I had seen.

When they killed her, they forgot about me. Their struggle had ended in victory, their campaign was over. With brutality that verged on madness, they threw us into the current. The queen was dead. The river took her quickly, and I hope mercifully, in that it was infinitely long, cold, and pure. I wished then that I would follow, but the river would not oblige.

Though it took her sadly and forever, it merely closed my wounds and stopped my bleeding. It roused me enough so that I knew to keep my head above water as I was carried downstream. It threw me against rocks, shocking me awake and into life. And soon I was floating at great speed through white water that I assumed would be the last thing I would know. The site of the battle was left behind so quickly and easily, with not a soldier or a horse to be seen, that I questioned memory and doubted my sanity as I choked on water, air, and sun.

Even infinite rivers need not be entirely straight, and this one took its turns where it wanted, wheeling left and right as it cut through cliffs or slowed to swirl around sparkling sandbars and in darkening pools. I was so cold that I could no longer feel my body and was pulled toward sleep, which is, I suppose, how one comes to terms with drowning slowly in a cold stream.

And then the river led me around a bend, the water slowed and warmed, and I was pushed into a deep still pool, where for days or weeks sun-heated water had risen to the surface and now was as hot as a bath. Here I stayed, slowly twirling, until I crawled out onto a bank of dry white sand. I slept and dreamt, and when I awoke I tried to stand. I pulled one leg toward my chest, then painfully pushed forward with my arms until I had one knee on the ground and my thigh upright. The other leg quickly followed suit, and I straightened myself. On my knees I was now high enough to see some distance down the sandbar, and after a few seconds I realized that not too far from me were tracks that started from the water's edge.

When finally I stood, shakily, I saw that they were hoofprints, and that the horse had been shod. What if, I thought ... what if the charger had turned over in the stream (after all, we might not have seen it) soon enough so that the baby had not drowned? Probably not, I thought. "Very unlikely," I said out loud even as I began to follow the tracks as fast as I could move. I knew from my own peculiar history that once I had begun something I rarely gave up, and I envisioned myself chasing a horse (which can, after all, find sustenance in grass) across an endless region of plains, forests, and mountains. Have you ever chased a horse even across a meadow?

Still, as I tried to weigh the sense of what I was doing I found myself doing it without cease, and never was there any possibility that I would break off. If the child had lived, he had to be saved. I owed his mother my life and more in the attempt, as I would any mother of any child. And if he had lived not only would I have a son and the queen smile in heaven, but the life of the kingdom would be saved.

The ground beyond the riverbed was hard and sometimes rocky, the trail difficult to follow, but I followed it even in moonlight, past moonlight into starlight, and past starlight to the dawn. I was hungry, aching, cold, and lame, and had no idea where I was going except up. The horse was interested in only one thing. He was a riser. He sought altitude.

Soon I too was rising, through steep forests, meadows, and onto snow-covered plateaux over which I could see the tracks in all light. I might even have been able to find them and follow had the stars been obliterated by cloud. The horse took every upward turn and made any choice to ascend. I found the climb exhausting and overpowering. A child may need me, I told myself, and not just a child, but the child of a woman that I deeply love still. And not just the child of the woman that I deeply love, but the king, into whose service I am sworn and to whom I owe even more than my life.

Now and then I had to sleep, although I tried not to, hoping to steal a march on the horse as he rested at night. I feared for the child, as the higher we went the colder it got, and he was carried across the snow with neither food nor water nor a heavy coverlet. After I had slept for a few minutes, I would force myself to go on, and this way I began to gain on the charger, whose tracks were looking

so fresh that had I only been unwounded enough to run I could have caught him in an hour.

And then after tracking them across a night of stars I saw them ahead of me in the rose light of dawn, drawing away on a vast mountain snowfield that was a world in itself. Rivers that the morning sun made red came hurtling from walls of granite the color of charcoal and silver. They floated through the air, braiding and untangling ribbons of white spray, slowly, politely, and without a sound. They came from so far up it was impossible to see where they started, and when they reached the foot of the cliffs they cut deep channels in the snow and ice and ran violently down the mountainside to water the world. This was the Veil of Snows.

For the first time in my life I saw the white wall, a mountain of light that looks like clean snow frothed in a punishing wind. It moves unpredictably to and fro, sometimes settling, sometimes receding, sometimes racing forward, and it roars. But even if you cannot hear yourself speak when you are half an hour's walk from the base, when you are close to it speech is the last thing on your mind.

The horse halted by a crescent in one of the rivers and stood calmly in the sunshine. He could not have been more than six of his own lengths from the wall, and fearing that it would come forward to swallow him up I began to run even though the running opened my wounds and overburdened my heart. In the bright light I had difficulty seeing, but I could make out the cradle, upright and sound, resting against the charger's side. As I got closer I saw a little arm suddenly thrust out from the cradle window beneath the overhang. I smiled. The little arm moved in the raw way that babies move, with quick and dictatorial energy. He was alive! All I had to do was get to him, take the bridle of the charger, and lead them down the mountain.

For fear of spooking the horse, I began to walk. Although I was cold and worn and my heart thundered in my chest, I walked slowly and confidently, trying to stay the horse from movement by imagining how I would seize the bridle. As I neared the horse I heard the baby's cry carried over the falling water.

I was close, almost there, and could see that this horse was in place until led away. Many different joys began to arise at once, but then, from out of the wall, in an instant, came a hundred bowmen and cavalry riding a hundred blood-colored horse of the Golden Horde. They were as dark as mahogany, and their eyes seemed unable to see this world. They looked past me, seeming to know exactly what they had come to do.

I was running and shouting, to no avail, and as I ran toward them I saw two women dismount and approach the cradle. They were smiling, and whereas I was moving as slowly as in a dream they were moving faster than I could believe. One lifted the overhang and the other took hold of the child. She raised him briefly above her toward the sun, and kissed him.

I was almost there, but I was caught in amber. They put him down on the snow, washed him in a matter of seconds, and wrapped him in a cloth redder than anything in nature. Although I desperately did not want them to take him, what they did seemed right and natural, and I was running as if in slow motion, crying out to people who seemed neither to see nor hear me, deafened by thunder, asking that it not be a dream.

The first woman mounted her horse and was given the baby. She strapped him to her front as the second woman went back to the cradle and took from it the queen's book wrapped in gold cloth. As they began to move back whence they had come, a man at the end

of the line appeared to notice me. He drew his short bow and put an arrow in it. As his horse walked him half disappearing into the wall, he aimed the arrow at me.

Clearly these people, with their sturdy and shaggy horses, their homes high in the ice world and close to the sun, their silent demeanor, and their otherworldly eyes, could have shot an arrow halfway around the world and hit whatever it was they were aiming for. I stopped, thinking that I was going to die, and as I watched the child recede, the threatening bowman simply stepped out of our time and into another. They were gone, and only the roar of the water and wall were left.

I approached the white front, which disappeared straight up as far as I could see, and as it seemed to be stable, oscillating only slightly as if in a technique for holding its place, I touched it with my finger. I felt nothing, and thrust in my arm, and then I realized that when the arm was inside it was gone, as if it had been dissolved a million years before, or had never existed. Inside, everything became even, all was nothing, and nothing was all. I could not imagine stepping in, perhaps to stay forever, or perhaps to find myself, washed clean, standing once again in this world.

How was it that the Golden Horde could enter and re-enter seemingly at will? And where was the child? Where was my queen? As these questions were too great for me, and still are, I stepped away. As I walked backward from the roar I tried to tell myself that it was all a dream. But then, after I turned, I saw the charger and the cradle, I touched them, I knew that it was real, and I began to lead the horse down the mountain. I did not enter the white fume, though someday, of course, I will, for I was the only one who knew the tale, and my duty, therefore, was to remain.

And so I have been here for twenty-five years, and though I have lost faith so often I cannot count the times, I have not lost faith at all, for in the bright of morning, just as I arise, I find my faith restored.

It is now against the law to say the name of the queen or her son, or even to hint at who they were. In all this time, you might think, I would have ceased to recall the surprising particulars, the warm smiles, the faces that eventually one cannot see anymore in photographs, as their stillness camouflages them against the passage of time and petrifies them in memory.

But I have not forgotten, for I believe in the unfolding of the tale, that, like water, it cannot be suppressed in its simple will to rise, if it is fed by rains and comes in abundance. The only thing that lasts is the unfolding of the tale, the only thing of which you can be sure.

Devotion becomes waiting, and waiting becomes devotion, and as I waited I became more certain, even though all logic conspired against it. And then this morning the bucket was blasted away on the stream. I have always drawn water from that bucket, and I had no other way of bringing water back to my room.

I walked slowly up the hill, and when I returned home I went out on my little mountaineer's balcony and watched the clear light from the east as it warmed the Veil of Snows. Then I began to write this tale. I could hardly keep up with it as it flooded from pen to page, perhaps because it had been waiting so long to be told, or perhaps because its only form was the simple truth.

For many hours under the bright sun I worked desperately hard and in the deepest concentration. I neither ate nor drank nor even moved, and time passed with such great speed that I seemed to finish only a moment after I had begun. Weak with hunger, exhaustion, and thirst, I fell asleep, and was awakened only when the sun crossed over the roof and left me in cool shadow. I was so hot I could barely get up, and I had to have water.

I went for the bucket automatically, but it was not there. Half awake and hardly able to walk, I felt that I was dreaming the end of things, or at least the end of me. Nothing seemed solid or true. I knew I could not walk down to the river again. I knew that I had never been as old or as weak, and that I had to have water.

In twenty-five years I hadn't touched the blue bottle. The water within was the past itself, and I had always promised that I would save it until the kingdom was restored. But I broke my promise, and dizzy and disoriented I abandoned my discipline and seized the bottle by its cobalt blue neck and took it out onto the balcony, where remnants of the morning heat radiated luxuriously from the wood.

Well, I thought, better that I drink it than some stranger after I'm gone. This was just a rationale for my weakness, but I was moved by something more than thirst. Though I was merely opening a bottle of water, I felt that I had betrayed all that I had believed in. I looked at it, amazed, as it bubbled after so long on the shelf and the light came perfectly through the blue. I smelled it, and it seemed to be fresher even than whitewater from the river.

This was the water of the old kingdom, and I drank it down. It was as good as on the day it had been bottled, and I came alive with regret, for I had not only lost faith, I had acted upon loss of faith, and now nothing was left.

So I threw the bottle high into the air, and it spun neck over base as it descended to the rocks and the river below, turning the water briefly into a shower of glistening blue as it shattered, its sinking

shards to be carried down to the plain, or perhaps just to settle in a cold black pool hidden somewhere within the trees.

Though I looked out at the Veil of Snows, prepared for deep sadness, what I saw was like an electric current that snapped through my body and danced in front of my eyes. Half the snowfields had turned as dark as mahogany, and the dark consumed the light as the Golden Horde marched down the mountainsides in a host larger than I had ever imagined, having switched allegiances, and come to our side, or so I prayed.

And, yes, it was so. In the lead of this army, as if tugging a shadow, were two immense columns that from a distance looked like braided threads. They were horsemen and soldiers in the colors red, of the father, and gold of the son, and though I had to look twice, and three times, and more, to tell myself that it was true, it was true, and I knew, and I would have known even had I not looked at all.

All this time, father and son had been in a place that I could not see, a place where I could not go, a place that I dared not imagine or wish for, in that it is the deepest desire of the human heart, and as we grow old we are taught not to wish for what we want. But in these years they had been together. And although I did not see her, I hoped that the queen, too, was hidden somewhere in the distant color of the march, though that may have been too much even to pray for.

For a moment they were obscured by the shadow of a cloud, and I thought that perhaps I was just an old man dreaming. But then the shadow lifted and I saw that the columns were close and real. And then I saw them, father and son, on the snowfields bright and near, riding together, as once they had done, in a kingdom far and clear.

MARK HELPRIN is one of the world's most celebrated living writers. His 11 works of fiction have been translated into more than 12 languages. A survey of writers and editors, published in *The New York Times Book Review* in May 2006, named his novel *Winter's Tale* among the best works of fiction of the past 25 years.

Published in *The New Yorker* for almost a quarter of a century, Mr. Helprin's stories and essays on politics and aesthetics also appear in *The Atlantic Monthly*, *The New Criterion*, *The Wall Street Journal*, *Commentary*, *The New York Times*, and many other international publications.

CHRIS VAN ALLSBURG is the winner of two Caldecott Medals, one for *The Polar Express* and one for *Jumanji*, which also won the 1982 National Book Award. He is also the recipient of a Caldecott Honor for *The Garden of Abdul Gasazi*. The author and illustrator of numerous picture books for children, he was awarded the Regina Medal for lifetime achievement in children's literature. Formerly an instructor at the Rhode Island School of Design, he lives in Rhode Island with his wife and two children.

A KINGDOM FAR AND CLEAR: THE COMPLETE SWAN LAKE TRILOGY

Printed and bound by Courier Corporation, Kendallville and Westford divisions

Text composed in Weiss, typeface designed by Emil Rudolf Weiss in 1924
Titles composed in Trajan Pro, typeface designed by Carol Twombly in 1989

Printed on 100# Utopia II Ivory
Signed, limited First Edition bound in dark blue Tocca Vivella, with matching slipcase
Second Edition bound in Arrestox B Navy Vellum